Unflinching

Unflinching

A Western

Stuart G. Yates

Published 2020 by Next Chapter
Base image courtesy of Magic Covers
Cover Design by The Cover Collection
Back cover texture by David M. Schrader, used under license from Shutterstock.com
Edited by D.S. Williams

Also by Stuart G. Yates

- Varangian
- Varangian 2 (King of the Norse)
- Burnt Offerings
- Whipped Up
- Splintered Ice
- The Sandman Cometh
- Roadkill
- Tears in the Fabric of Time

Acknowledgements and Dedication

As with any work of fiction, there are so many people to thank, for their support and belief in what I try to do. For all the staff at Next Chapter, a huge thank you for your faith; for Elmore Leonard and Robert B Parker, for inspiring me to write a Western which is relative to our world; and to my friends who have always been there, but, for this one, most especially to my best friend, Ray. We've seen so many Westerns together and enjoyed every one. I hope he enjoys this, for it is for him.

One

They swung the wagon down into the tiny side street, which ran alongside the store. Randall pulled on the wheel-brake and gave a long sigh. Stained with sweat and dust, his shirt stuck to his back and when he pulled off his hat, tangled hair clung tight to his scalp. The thick, acrid air sucked all the moisture from everything, including himself, but now, having reached his destination, the first signs of relief trickled through his bones and the strain left his features. He smiled across to Elisabeth who sat stoically beside him, eyes straight ahead. She said, "Is this finally it?"

He was in awe of her composure, how she remained so elegant despite the rigors of the past weeks. "It is." He reached over and patted her knee. "The worst is over now."

She turned. "Can you be sure?"

"We got through those Indians, didn't we?" He kissed her lightly on the cheek. "We can relax now, turn our mind to normal things."

"Like the things we used to concentrate on."

"Precisely." He replaced his hat. "I'll go and get some supplies then call on the sheriff, see if he can point us in Widow Langton's direction."

"I have a bad feeling about all of this. Why didn't she answer any of our correspondence?"

"There'll be a genuine reason, I'm sure."

"Maybe she's sold her place to someone else."

"I doubt it. My lawyer drew up the deeds. She'd be a fool if she did that. I don't believe she's a fool, and her family connections over in Illinois stand as security. It'll be fine."

"Well maybe she's dead."

He gave Elisabeth an understanding look, conscious of her anxiety, of being so close to a new life. The trail had proven hard, the recent drought one of the longest ever known. People out on the plains were struggling to survive, settlers and natives both. Desperation led to excesses on both sides, brought out the very worst in people. But this town, with its fine buildings and well-ordered streets gave a sense of hope. He wished she would accept it. "Honey, there'll be an honest explanation for why she didn't return my cable. Communication is spasmodic at best in this part of the country. Maybe the lines went down, who knows? We'rc out west now and we have to get used to the fact that life here is different."

"Primitive is what you mean."

He smiled. "We've talked about all this – it's only natural to have these self-doubts. We're taking the first steps on a brand new life, with all its uncertainties, but it's exciting too. Once we're in our new place, have settled in, got into a routine, everything will seem a lot brighter. I promise."

"I know." She looked around her, to the wooden buildings on either side of the quiet street, then craned her neck towards the main drag. "I hate to say it again, but it just seems so… *primitive.* It's nothing like Chicago, that's for sure."

"These towns, they are new, maybe only been here for a few years. Now that the rush is over, it'll take time to readjust, to create new, longer lasting opportunities. We're at the forefront of that, Elisabeth. Pioneers."

"Or what are those other name they give us – tenderfoots? Sodbusters?"

It'll be okay," he reassured her, gathered himself and jumped down onto the dirt. "You wanna come with me?"

"No. Just don't be too long in there. When you're done, we'll go to the sheriff's together and get the legalities moving."

Always his little lawyer, his rock. He smiled and tramped down the street.

One or two people acknowledged him, but for the most part the street was quiet. Opposite him ran a group of stores, a small hotel and a telegraph office with a bank squeezed in between. A milliners took his attention and he thought about buying Elisabeth a new hat. After the visit to the sheriff perhaps, after the papers were signed and they were both feeling more reassured, they could take some time, get their bearings. Buy things. He knew in his heart this was a good move, the *right* move. A fine ranch, with a dozen acres of good grazing land, sweet water, space to grow. The land registry had assured him the purchase was sound. Widow Langton was an honest woman, the lawyers said so and Randall knew it. The time for doubts and uncertainties was gone. They were here, safe, unharmed; the first day of the rest of their lives.

He stepped up onto the boardwalk and doffed his hat as two ladies in fine bonnets and trailing dresses drifted by. They smiled in return, a simple gesture, but one which caused his heart to swell. Buoyed up, he clumped along towards the hardware store, crossing the window fronts of the small bank and the telegraph office – which would come in handy for when he needed to send a message to his sister back east that all was well. He recalled how forlorn and concerned she'd looked, standing on the station platform, tiny handkerchief pressed to her mouth, her other hand waving. Elisabeth had cried. So did he.

But that was then and life changed from the moment they alighted the train. The purchase of the wagon and horse, supplies, listening to the stern words of advice from the proprietor of the hardware store. Two old prospectors joined in. Reading between the words, it was clear none gave father and daughter much chance of surviving. The trail was hard, unforgiving, with many dangers along the way. He'd need to shoot, they all advised, and Randall could shoot. The proprietor didn't seem convinced and the two old men laughed. A week into their journey, when the Indians came out of the dust, with their intent clearly visible in their scowls and nocked bows, Randall blew them out of their saddles, no questions asked. A pity nobody back at the store had witnessed it. Their low opinion of Randall may have been somewhat upgraded. He shook his head, pushing such thoughts to one side, took off his hat and went through the door of the store.

There were a couple of young women in the far corner, giggling as they sifted through a large catalogue. One of them glanced over to him and caught his eye before she looked away, cheeks reddening, and nudged her friend, who checked him out and smiled.

Randall nodded and stepped over to the counter. He was a lean, rangy man who moved with the grace and easy stride of a big cat. His forearms rippled with muscle, the skin tanned. A hard life, close friends with death, made him tough, resilient. For twenty-five years he'd followed his father's path through the military; now the time was here for him to pursue a new path, and with his wife Caroline passing away, nothing remained to hold him back. He tipped his hat at the girls and they giggled again.

He pushed the bell, and within a few moments, a trim, middle-aged woman emerged through a beaded curtain. She was small, dressed in a tight black dress, hair pulled back into a bun, showing off her handsome features to good effect. Her face, pale and serious, gave nothing away as she studied him from head to foot. "We don't give credit."

Randall blinked, shooting a glance towards the girls, who both laughed. He coughed. "I, er, don't intend to ask for any, ma'am."

"Well that's good. I always like new customers to know where they stand before any purchases are considered." She frowned and Randall stared back, face blank. "Before they *buy*, that is my meaning. That way there cannot be any misunderstanding."

"Yes, quite understandable. But I have money. I need some grain for my horse and," he looked down and tugged at the threadbare knees of his pants, "some work clothes. We've been on the trail for something like three weeks and we're both in desperate need of something new to wear."

She nodded, pointing vaguely behind him, "There's a selection of items behind you. Both of you, you said."

"Yes. My daughter is with me."

"I see. Well, ladies' clothes are somewhat more difficult to acquire, but as you can see, we have a catalogue." The girls giggled again, whispering to one another. "If you're planning on settling, that is."

"Indeed we are. We have purchased Widow Langton's place."

"Have you indeed? Well, that's a right tidy spread, built up by her good husband before the fever took him. "

"She is still alive then? I was hoping the sheriff might—"

"Oh, she's alive. No question. She boards at Drayton's, just a way along Main Street, second on the left. Nice place. She seems happy." She frowned. "What might you be needing the sheriff for?"

"Pay my respects, prepare some papers, that sort of thing. As we're strangers here I thought it best to introduce myself to the town officials before settling into our new place."

"Well, Sheriff Pickles will no doubt help you with the formalities an' all. Can't say I know what those formalities might be, but we are a friendly town. Treat people right and they'll treat you the same. No doubt we will be seeing you in church on Sunday?"

"Of course." He smiled and reached inside his pocket. He brought out an ancient leather wallet, which almost fell apart when he opened it. He extracted a dollar bill. "This is for the grain. I'll take a look at those clothes."

She smiled, an action which changed the entire complexion of her face. Her features relaxed, any nervous tension slipping away as she picked up the money and put it into a drawer underneath the counter.

Randall was about to say something when from out in the street, a voice cried out in alarm, quickly followed by a series of gunshots. The girls in the corner shrieked and one of them stumbled backwards, falling into a shelving unit, which gave way under her weight and collapsed. The storekeeper clamped her hands over her mouth and more yells and shouts echoed through the street. "Oh my, that must be the bank!"

Randall's only thought was for Elisabeth, still sitting outside on the wagon. He had no idea what caused the mayhem outside, but he wasn't about to expose his daughter to any danger, especially not the kind that involved shooting. He crossed the store in three quick bounds and tore open the door.

He squinted into the sunlight. There were people running along the street, horses were bucking and neighing loudly close by and as he looked to his left, he saw them; two men, neckerchiefs over their mouths and noses, brandishing heavy-looking firearms, one of them bleeding from the arm, the other holding a canvas bag which appeared weighty in his fist.

Two others erupted from the bank, revolvers barking in all directions, mainly skywards. Randall suspected their intention was to frighten, not harm. He instinctively reached for his hip, and swore when he remembered his own Army Colt was back in the wagon, together with a single shot carbine. With Elisabeth.

Randall wanted nothing to do with these men and made his decision to get as far away as fast as he could. As he went to move towards the side street where he'd parked the wagon, Elisabeth came tearing around the corner towards him, hair and eyes wild. He wanted to shout out, tell her to stop, return to the wagon, but his words became lost as a large, pot-bellied man charged from out of a building opposite, firing off a series of shots from his handgun.

Bullets zipped and cracked overhead, forcing Randall to dive face first to the boardwalk. He clamped his hands over his head, straining his neck to catch a glimpse of Elisabeth, holding her tresses, pressing herself against the side of the general store. She slid down to the wooden slats, screaming. She was in shock.

"Stay down," screamed Randall as another bullet smacked in the woodwork above where he lay. Did the buffoon with the handgun think he was one of the robbers?

He didn't receive an answer. One of the real robbers, standing a few paces away from him, fired his revolver, and hit the big man in the chest, throwing him down into the dirt. He lay there on his back, blood seeping from the wound. The robber ran across the street, sweeping up the man's gun and looked back. "Nathan, get to the God-damned horses!"

All hell was breaking loose. People, some of them armed, were appearing from all areas of the street, many shouting, most looking on and seeming petrified. The third and fourth robbers were blazing away with their firearms, some of the townspeople returning fire. The smell of hot lead filled the afternoon air, bullets slapping into woodwork, pinging off metal stanchions, or fizzing overhead.

"Get the hell out," screamed the first robber. Randall got to his knees and watched him levelling his revolver at the stricken man in the street. Without any outward show of hesitation or conscience, the robber blew the man's head apart from point-blank range. A collective wail rang out across the street and the majority of the onlookers stampeded in every direction. The killer whirled and his eyes settled on something across the street from where he stood.

Randall climbed to his feet and swayed, uncertain, light-headed. He saw Elisabeth standing frozen, ashen, eyes unable to take in such horrors, tears streaming down her face. He took a step towards her, dismissive of the danger all around.

"Mason, grab that wagon and get off the damned street!"

The panic welled up from within Randall's gut. The killer must have spotted the wagon, and now meant to take it and escape, with all that meant for father and daughter. With no possessions, the new life he'd dreamed for them both would be undermined before it began. Randall could not allow such a thing. He took another step, then something as heavy as a blacksmith's anvil slammed into his back and he pitched forward onto his face once more. The world flipped all around him, everything skewed, senses confused, head spinning. From far away, Elisabeth screamed and Randall, unable to understand, or move watched as a man's feet stepped over him and strode towards her. Randall tried to raise himself up, move the weight from his back, but he couldn't. The strength was leaving him, leaving him quickly. He saw the man taking Elisabeth around the waist, lifting her. She was kicking, struggling, but the man was too strong.

"Get her in the wagon, God-damn you!"

Another robber appeared in view. He spotted Randall, seemed to be considering something before a gunshot rang out, the bullet taking him high up in the arm. He groaned, staggered to the side and hit the building with a grunt. Three, four, five more shots hit him in the chest and stomach, the blood blooming like red-roses across his body. He crumpled, died.

"Oh no, Nathan!"

With the clouds parting in his head, the sunshine burst through and Randall's brain pieced together the details, although the pain in his back burned and the muscles in his legs refused to work. But he saw them. He saw the first robber, the killer of pot-belly, stooping beside his dead companion as the other two struggled with Elisabeth, who kicked and screamed. They were taking her to the wagon, for God-knows-what awful reason. If only he had a gun. If only he'd thought. He groaned, tears sprouting, frustration overwhelming him. For it all to end here, in this nameless street, after the life he'd had. Dear God, where was the justice in that? And Elisabeth. *Please, don't take her from me!*

The robber was on his feet. He held two guns, one spent, hammer clicking on empty cylinders. A bullet struck him in the throat and he went down, gurgling. Randall heard the sound of a whip cracking. They had the wagon. *Oh no, please, please!*

More gunshots. Randall thought he saw money floating in the breeze. Crisp dollar bills. Was any of it real, or a dream? He didn't know, his only desire was to be able to stand, to walk, to rush to Elisabeth's side. He heard another scream, but more distant this time. A cry of "*Father!*" More gunshots. Oh God…

A quiet voice came to him from out of the confusion, a cool hand on his neck. He turned. Black clouds were settling over the town. A storm was coming. He saw her in the gloom, the storekeeper, her face so lovely, but gripped by anguish.

"Dear God, mister. Hold on, hold on. We'll get a doctor."

Why would he need a doctor? All he needed was to get to his feet, stop those horrible men from manhandling his Elisabeth.

"Please," he said. He wanted to say more, to tell them to rescue his daughter, to apprehend the robbers. At least he wanted to say those things, but for some reason he didn't have the strength. So he turned his head, lay his cheek against the cool of the boardwalk and breathed through his mouth. No strength now. No worries. His one remaining desire, to sleep.

Two

The office rang with confused voices as Simms came in from out of the rain, shaking himself like a dog.

"Jeez, Simms!" Henson brushed spots of rainwater from his paperwork. He sat behind a desk not two paces from the door, spectacles pushed back on his head, shirtsleeves rolled up almost to his shoulders. He seemed frazzled, hair wild, as if it had dried in a mid-season hurricane.

"What's with all the panic?" Simms threw his coat and hat across the back of his chair and sat down.

"Got a telegram, not twenty minutes ago," said Henson, scouring through his papers, not looking up. "Seems like General Tobias J. Randall got himself caught up in a bank robbery in some lice-ridden backwater over on the Colorado-Utah border. His daughter's been kidnapped."

Simms rested his elbows on his desk, put his face in his hands and groaned. "And they sent for us?"

"As a retired, former general, he comes under Federal jurisdiction, but it seems they have had little success in tracking him."

"Great."

Henson looked up, measuring Simms with quiet indifference. Simms looked at him from between his fingers. Henson tilted his head sideways and asked, "Why are you so pissed?"

"Because I know Randall, so it's highly likely I'll get the assignment."

"You *know* him? How the hell do you know General Tobias J. Randall?"

"I served under him in the war with Mexico, at Churubusco back in '47. I was part of Clarke's Brigade. It was all a long, long time ago."

"I never knew you were a soldier."

"Lieutenant." Simms dropped his hands. "I never thought I'd need to do this sort of nonsense again."

"Well, you never know, Simms. They may not even give you the assignment. For all you know they may already have someone else to—"

At that moment, an office door in the far reaches of the room was wrenched open and a large, burly man sweating profusely and sporting enormous side whiskers, peered out into the room. He caught sight of Simms and growled, "Where the hell have you been?"

"I was feeling sick, so I decided to—"

"Get yourself in here *now*, Simms. You have a job to do."

The door crashed shut and Simms turned and gave Henson a knowing look. "You were saying?"

Henson looked away and Simms sighed. He shoved his chair back, edged his way through the bustle around him, and went through the office door without knocking.

"It's a helluva place," said Chesterton, leaning back in his chair, which creaked alarmingly. Before him, he'd laid out a large map of the Territories. "That's why I chose you. You know what it's like."

"I've never been to Utah."

"No, but you've served, and with some distinction so I understand. You know how to survive and the only way we're going to get the good General's daughter back is by cutting across that hellhole and tracking her down." He pointed to the map. "Most of it is uncharted, although there is the trail, of course. Nevertheless, you'll need wits, skill and a large helping of luck."

"I'm not a tracker, sir. I can shoot, I can fight, I can lay down in a hole and stay there for three days without moving, but I'm no tracker."

"Then find yourself someone who is. I hear there's a lot of Indians out there."

"There's a lot of everything out there. And some of those Indians are mean. They hate us."

"Yes, but as you say, you're a survivor. Three days in a hole might be just the thing. Listen," he came forward, planting his arms on the desk, covering the map, and peered straight into Simms's eyes. "I'm not going to lie to you; this is one of the toughest assignments we've had, but if we are to make any headway in this business, we need something to grab the headlines, shake up the powers-that-be in Washington. They sent two Federal Marshalls over there, and they never came back. Disappeared."

"Perhaps they got lost."

Chesterton shook his head. "No. Their bodies were eventually found by some settlers, who took 'em back to Laramie. Pegged out in the dirt they were, roasted black by the sun, their cocks stuffed in their mouths."

"Nice."

"Mr. Pinkerton met with the President." He paused, waiting for a reaction. Simms remained stoic and Chesterton sighed. "The President was convinced by Mr. Pinkerton's assertion that we are the finest law-enforcement agency there is, and only we could deliver. Consequently, we've been given the assignment, Simms, and you are the man for the job. You'll travel over to Wyoming, which I think is the furthest west you can go from here, then make your way across the Territories until you find her."

"And if she's dead?"

"The remit is to find her. Nobody said anything about finding her either dead or alive."

"I need men, sir. At least three."

Chesterton shook his head. "Can't spare 'em. Nor can the government. Seems it's ugly over there, Simms, talk of a war. Them Mormons..." He shook his head. "Brigham Young has got a cracker up his ass about folk over at Bridger selling whiskey to the Indians. He might be right, but it's leading to all sorts of conflict. That's the place you're going to Simms. A war zone."

"And to think I was actually contemplating taking today off."

"I'd have hauled you in anyway." Chesterton opened a drawer in his desk and pulled out a small wooden box, which he flipped open, extracted a cigar and rolled it under his nose.

Simms frowned and stood up. He felt very tired all of a sudden. "I'll get my things together. "

"You do this right, Simms. I don't want to see you back in this office without the girl, you get me? Randall is a national hero and those bastards who took his daughter, they need dealing with. You understand?"

"So, it's a rescue and assassination mission?"

"Phrase it however you want, just get it done."

He threw the box back into his drawer, leaned back and put a match to the cigar. He sucked on it furiously.

"You need to cut it," suggested Simms, "in order to smoke it."

Chesterton's eyes narrowed. "Just get the fuck out of my office, you pompous bastard."

Simms did just that.

Sometime later, Simms waited in the rain at the main ticket office, whilst the clerk behind the grill tapped his teeth with a pencil as he trailed a finger down a printed piece of paper. He clicked his tongue, shook his head, and appeared miserable. "Sorry, sir, there is nothing that gets you even close. Fort Laramie is about the nearest, but then you'd have to either board another train to Fort Bridger, or get a stage, if there is one. I doubt it though. It's a fairly wild place, mister. Lots of trouble over there, with Mormons and the like." He looked up, "Either way, it'll be up to you, but I reckon your best bet would be to get yourself a horse at Bridger. If it's still there, of course. You never can tell in this day and age."

Simms sighed, chewed his thoughts around for a moment, and finally put a five-dollar bill on the small counter. "Fort Laramie will be just fine."

The official wrote out the ticket and slid it under the grill, together with a few coins in change. Simms folded the ticket and put it away under his coat. He turned, looking to the sky, the clouds heavy and leaden, the rain well set for the rest of the day.

He wondered if it would be raining where he was headed.

Somehow, he doubted it, but he knew a lot worse things than rain waited for him out in the Territory.

Three

He slept most of the way, the rhythmic movement of the train helping him rest, oblivious to the rolling landscape, the changing scenery, the weather gradually growing brighter, and much hotter. When the train lurched and slowed down, he stirred and found himself sitting opposite two grizzled old men swathed in black coats, faces covered with tangled beards, their stares disturbingly piercing. Simms stretched and pressed his face against the window, anxious to gain his bearings. He saw nothing he recognized so he turned hopefully to the men opposite. "Do either of you two gentlemen know where we are?"

A passenger across the aisle leaned forward. "They don't understand you, sir. They're French."

Simms frowned, looked from the passenger back to the two Frenchmen. He sighed, shot the man a glance. "Do *you* know where we are?"

"Moving through Nebraska, but the line stops in about ten or so miles."

"It does?" Simms shuffled uncomfortably in the hard seat. "I thought it went as far as Fort Laramie?"

"Well, if the line reaches that far, I doubt it'll be this train. Best ask at the station when we get there. Perhaps there is some sort of connecting service."

Simms nodded and studied the other passenger. He was well-dressed in a brown, tweed suit, brogue tan shoes and a Derby hat sat by his side. Clean-shaven, middle-aged, he looked every inch a city banker, or someone similar. "Name's Nathaniel Constantine," he said, prompted by Simms's gaze, and thrust out his hand.

"Please to meet you," said Simms, shaking the man's hand. The grip was dry, firm. "My name is Simms. I'm making my way to Utah, to meet up with some business associates."

"Ah, yes." Constantine nodded knowingly. "Some fine opportunities out there, so I understand. I'm in the poultry business myself, looking to establish a network of chicken farms in this area. My company is assured of success, given the number of people now settling in and around the Territory. What business might you be in?"

Simms remained calm. He'd never suspected he might need a cover story. "Livery. For the Government. I'm instructed to buy horses for the Army."

"Ah, that'll be because of the trouble brewing in Utah. Yes, we've all heard about that. Nasty business."

"Yes indeed." Simms shifted his gaze to take in the view through the carriage window. The sun beat down on an endless plain, punctuated by rocky outcrops but little else, the distant hills forming a backdrop to the vista. "It sure looks dry."

"Oh, it is. It hasn't rained for days, even weeks. Some say if it continues, crops might fail. Settlers will be in for a hard season."

"Doesn't bode well for your chickens." Simms twisted around to see Constantine's expression faltering.

"Well… they do say the situation is far worse in Colorado. People are starving, so I hear. Perhaps they might move back once they hear of my company's plan."

"You could be right," Simms said and forced a smile. The two Frenchmen were no longer staring. Both had pulled their hats over their eyes and were sleeping. Simms settled himself into his seat and tried to do the same.

He sprang up, roused by a violent shaking of his shoulder. Constantine loomed over him, flashing his grin. "We're here, Mr. Simms. I wish you well in your endeavors."

Grunting, Simms stood up, reaching up to the rack where his portmanteau waited. "Thank you. You too, Mr. Constantine."

He noted the Frenchmen were no longer there. With a grunt he pulled down his case and made his way out onto the platform.

The heat hit him like a wall, forcing him to stop on the bottom step. He took a moment before striding across the wooden platform to the tiny office. The locomotive sizzled and snorted behind him, other passengers drifting away. He saw Constantine talking to a man beside a rickety-looking carriage, pulled by the thinnest, most moth-eaten mule he thought he'd ever seen. This place was certainly in the doldrums, he mused, and went straight to the ticket booth.

From within the booth, a tired weasel of a man sauntered up to the grill. He looked hot, close to death, gnarled hands running across his brow.

"I need to get to Fort Bridger," said Simms without preamble, "or as close as I can get."

"We do have a train to Fort Laramie," the little man wheezed, "but it only calls once every two weeks." He pulled a face. "You missed it by three days."

"Once every two weeks?" Simms blew out his cheeks, swiveled around on his heels and surveyed the surroundings. "Is there a stage?"

"Sometimes. Best going into town…"

"And buying myself a horse. Yes, I've heard all that. Thanks."

"…best going into town and asking at the hardware store. Man there name of Buster Norwich owns a half share in the local stagecoach. He's the man to ask."

"Where will I find this hardware store?"

"It's on the main drag. You can't miss it."

Simms doffed his hat, hefted his portmanteau, and drifted away.

It took him five or more minutes to stroll towards the town. It was a mixed bag of weather-beaten, rundown stores and hotels, and newer, fresher looking cattle association offices. He moved through the almost-deserted main street, aware of people's stares, and spotted the hardware store at the far end. As he moved closer, he noticed a man standing next to the doorway, arms folded, appearing bored. He studied Simms's approach for a few moments before turning and disappearing inside.

Simms paused and took another look around the street. Very few bystanders remained. A slight tickle played around the nape of his neck, the same sort which always manifested itself when he was about to go into action. With a growing sense of unease, he clumped across the sidewalk and went inside the store. A tiny bell shrilled to announce his entrance. Simms took a moment to survey the interior. The single room was a jumble of every conceivable type of merchandise available for settlers, builders, cow-herders, perhaps even bounty-hunters, because there were guns. Lots of them. He wandered over to a rack of smooth bore muskets, together with a choice offering of rifled carbines. He picked one up, worked the mechanism.

From the corner of his eye, Simms spotted the man who had stood in the doorway, coming through a beaded curtain behind a large counter. Gruff looking, massive shoulders, ruby-red face, he coughed. Simms, making as if this was the first inkling he had of the man's entrance, stiffened slightly and turned. He hefted the carbine. "Nice piece."

The man glared. "Can I help you?"

"I hope so." Simms returned the carbine to its place and crossed to the counter. He took off his hat. "I hear there might be a stage to Fort Laramie?"

"You just got in off the train." Simms nodded. "Well, about the stage, you heard wrong."

"Oh. I understood you—"

"Are you buying?"

"No, I want to get to Fort Laramie. I was hoping you'd be able to—"

"If you ain't buying, I'll be asking you to leave."

Simms rocked back on his heels, blew out a silent whistle. "Mister, I'm not here to cause trouble. I have business in Laramie and need to get there. I was informed, by the good man at the railroad station, that you ran a stage. I'm merely asking—"

"Stage hasn't run out of here for over six months, mister. Too much nonsense in the Territories. If you're aiming to head for Laramie, my suggestion is to buy a horse."

"And where might I do that?"

"'Round back." He jerked his thumb towards the rear of the building. "There's a livery stable there. They'll give you a good offer for a horse and rig. Also, where you're going, you'll need firearms."

Simms nodded, unbuttoned his coat and pushed it away to reveal the pistols already holstered around his person.

Buster Norwich, or so Simms assumed the man to be, studied the guns, smirked, then turn his head, hawked and spat on the floor. "Damned bounty-hunters. Your business in Laramie got something to do with taking a few scalps, trading off some innocents for desperadoes? Jesus, you make me sick." He reached under the counter and brought up a shotgun, barrels sawn off. But if he had a desire to use the weapon, or merely to intimidate, he did not get very far. Before he could bring the impressive firearm to bear, Simms pulled out the Colt Dragoon at his hip and rapped the barrel hard across the big man's nose, sending him screaming and squirming to the ground, collapsing into the well-stocked shelves behind him. The suddenness and weight of his fall brought down a profusion of cans, bottles and paper bags, filled with an assortment of flour and maize, around his head.

Simms holstered his revolver, returned to the rifle rack and lifted out the carbine he'd been looking at. Recognizing it from his War days, Simms hefted the weapon in his hands. An Eighteen-forty-three model, Halls breechloading carbine. A fine gun. Grinning, he vaulted the counter, and scraped around, searching for cartridges. He found a small carton, only half-full of ready-made paper cartridges, and dropped them into his pocket. He kicked the shotgun away well out of reach, stomped his foot into the writhing man's groin for good measure, and went through the beaded curtain, carbine in hand.

The rear door yawned wide open. Beyond it, Simms could just make out a battered old barn, surrounded on two sides by a makeshift fence. A broken cart lay next to the entrance. He did not step closer so the angle from which he looked obscured most of the details, but he could see enough to realize this was no livery stable. A miserable attempt to waylay him, perhaps, with Norwich's associates standing just out of sight, waiting.

He turned and went back into the shop. He stooped down beside Norwich and put the end of the barrel under the squirming man's chin. "You aiming to kill me, boy?" he asked through gritted teeth.

Norwich, eyes cloudy with tears, blabbed, shaking his head. "Please," was all he managed.

"How did you know I was coming?"

To lend some weight to his question, he pushed the barrel deeper into Norwich's thick throat. He gagged. "Seamus."

"And who is he?"

"We have a deal. He sends tenderfoots over here, to ask about the stage." Sobs broke out from his slack mouth, the tears tumbling down his face. "Don't kill me, please."

"The guy at the railroad station?" Simms stood up. "Jesus, you people. How many have you waylaid this way?"

Norwich, unable to answer, curled himself up into a ball, bleating like a lamb.

"Too damned many, that's for sure." Simms scooped up the shotgun, broke it open and dropped the cartridges to the floor. He then took to smashing the gun on the counter edge before tossing the ruined weapon into the far corner. "How many are waiting for me out back?"

Norwich dragged in a shuddering breath. "Only one, Johnny-boy. A kid. Don't hurt him."

Simms narrowed his eyes. "One? That means there are at least two, and they ain't no kids."

"What you gonna do?"

"Get myself a horse."

He moved quick, running out of the store, back into the sunlight. Main Street remained as quiet as ever, which might be a problem, but Simms was sufficiently experienced in this sort of thing to know that as soon as the gunfire broke out, people would keep their heads down.

So he continued to run, taking the passageway, which ran down the side of the store, and stopped at the corner.

He listened. A couple of horses neighed, kicking at the ground, but nothing else. He estimated the distance between where he stood and the rear entrance to the store. Perhaps fifteen paces, maybe less. He checked the carbine, brought it up to his eye line, and stepped around the corner.

As he suspected, they were either side of the doorway. The nearest one, with his back to him, was a lumbering slob of a man, wearing a sweat-stained white shirt, hanging like a tent around his frame. A ten-gallon perched on his head; he was a true caricature the people back east believed those out west to be. He held a large, heavy-looking bat in his hand, his breathing labored. Simms could hear the wheeze grow louder as he inched closer.

Simms drew in a quiet breath, took a line on the man's calf muscles, and squeezed the trigger.

The carbine boomed in the stillness of the afternoon, the bullet slapping into the big man's leg, whipping it out from under him to dump him unceremoniously on his huge behind. He squealed, more from shock than anything, and clamped both hands over the bullet wound in his calf, writhing in the dirt as the blood spewed from between his fingers.

His partner, who stood opposite with a rusted spade in both hands, saw Simms and went white. He dropped his weapon, and took two or three steps backwards. He gibbered something incomprehensible and wet his pants. Appalled, he turned and sprinted away in the opposite direction. Simms let him go, not wanting to kill any of these amateur bush-whackers. News would soon get around, he hoped. Future visitors to this shit-hole town would be more aware of the sort of welcome awaiting them.

He opened the breech, fed a new cartridge into the carbine and waited, keeping one eye on the moaning man on the ground, who rolled around clutching his shattered leg. If he didn't get it fixed, he could be dead within a few days, Simms mused. He had seen it all too often, with soldiers on the battlefield receiving little more than a glancing wound but succumbing to a raging fever well after the fighting ended. More men died from wounds than from the field of battle, he knew that. He didn't profess to understand the reasons why. Perhaps someone, some day, would figure it out.

The horses were spooked, rearing up, screeching, desperate to escape from the ropes binding them to a hitching rail next to the ramshackle old barn. The structure groaned, shaking dangerously from side to side. He needed to act quickly. Another shot would have the horses tearing themselves free and stampeding off into the distance, so when Norwich appeared in the doorway, one of the smooth bore muskets primed in his hands, Simms reached for the knife under his right arm and, in one smooth, flowing movement, sent it slicing through the air. The blade hit Norwich in the chest, with such force it sank almost to the hilt. Norwich gaped at the offending implement in total shock, the musket dropping from numbed fingers. He teetered backwards and fell down amongst the clutter of his rear storeroom. His feet twitched and a horrible gurgling sound bubbled up in his throat. Simms stepped over the writhing big man with the wounded leg and dipped his long frame into the storeroom. He stared into Norwich's wide-open eyes.

"I never meant for anyone to get hurt," Norwich jabbered, confusion and incomprehension over what had occurred mingling together. He clenched his teeth. "Oh Jesus, I never meant to hurt you."

"No, you just meant to stove my head in with a baseball bat. You're a genuine do-gooder, Norwich." Simms bent down, gripped the handle of the knife, and tore it free. Norwich screamed and Simms wiped the bloody blade on the stricken man's shirt. "You'll be dead within the hour, so make your peace with God, you miserable bastard."

"Help me."

Simms tilted his head. "Like you would have helped me, I suppose?" He stood up and went back outside, leaving Norwich to gurgle and wheeze. He should really pay a visit to the guy back at the railroad station, bring some retribution down on his head, but he thought better of it. Time was pressing, but at least he had an empty store to rummage through. He would leave money for anything he needed for the journey and write a receipt and payment for the horse on the counter. This might delay any lynch-hungry posse from following his trail. But he doubted it.

He sighed. This was all so unnecessary and was not how he wanted this assignment to start out. Life always played its hand in the most unexpected of ways. He knew this, but the knowledge didn't make it any less difficult to swallow.

He moved as cautiously as he could towards the horses.

Four

He didn't stop riding until he reached a mountain range, a narrow trail taking him high up into its interior, discovering a cave where he camped, fed his horse and stretched himself out to sleep.

The sun dropped low behind the horizon. Across the vast sky a single eagle swooped, its plaintive call a mirror to the stark loneliness of the mountains. Anything that lived here scratched out a sorry existence. The arid land was hard, unrelenting, the lack of rain a killer. He'd seen it on the ride, prairie dogs and coyotes, even birds sometimes, lying in tangled heaps, bodies twisted and blackened, baked hard by the heat.

He'd filled two canteens with water back at the town, and barely half of one still held liquid inside. If he didn't find another town, farm or homestead soon to replenish his dwindling supplies, he'd be just another dried up corpse out on the prairie. He feared most for his horse. If she succumbed, his chances of survival would be virtually nil.

Damn this land and damn this assignment. It would have been better to travel across to San Francisco, make his base there, get properly supplied, drum up some help. Out here, alone, he was vulnerable to any number of would-be attackers, human and animal. He checked his pockets. He had five cartridges left for his new carbine. Five. If a posse of twelve came after him, how many could he feasibly pick off before they surrounded and dangled his neck from the nearest tree?

Given such a scenario, he mused, casting an eye across the plain, there wasn't a single tree in sight. A bullet in the brain might serve equally as well, before they propped his body up against a cliff face with a sign around his neck, 'Horse thief and killer'. Great end to an otherwise mediocre career. He sighed, stretched his arms high above his head and decided from now on he would travel through the night, when it was cooler. He looked at his horse. She too, would fare better in the coolness of the night. And if he came across a homestead, then he'd camp and wait until morning, for he did not wish to spook any people he might meet. *If* he came across anything. In this vast, blighted land, he may just as easily find nothing at all. He sighed, pulled his blanket tight around his throat and tried to sleep.

* * *

Franklyn Phelps was a small man; his stick thin arms and scraggily neck akin to a turkey's, causing many to wonder about his age and his health. Perhaps he was dying of some hideous disease, but many commented on the fact he'd always appeared this way. When he was a boy, his playmates would call him weed, or piss-pants because he constantly carried with him an overpowering stench of urine. Back then, some said that was also because he was sick. Now, a grown man, it seemed Franklyn Phelps wore his sickness like a label around his neck. Whatever the sickness was.

He prodded Norwich's dead body and screwed up his lips, ruminating on what might have happened.

"What we gonna do?"

He strained his neck to measure Dan Parks with a dark stare. "What would you have me do, Dan? Send out smoke signals perhaps?"

"We could hunt the bastard," suggested another, larger man, meaner than a skunk with a red-hot poker up his backside.

"Hunt who exactly, Stolen? Tobias didn't get a look at him as he high-tailed it out of town, and Johnny-boy Fletcher is battling for his life with his legs all blown to shit. Nobody knows who he is."

Stolen shrugged. "We could follow his trail."

"Oh, and ride straight into a bunch of Indians? No thank you."

"Well, we can't just let the bastard get away with it," hawked Parks. "I mean; what sort of a *smoke* signal does that send out?"

Stolen nodded enthusiastically, adding, "Seamus over at the rail station will know him. He's the one who sent him over here in the first place."

"Over the past year, Seamus Rogers has sent twenty or more poor bastards over here to Norwich, to relieve them of their wares." Phelps sighed, studying Norwich once more. "Seems like their profitable line of business has run its course."

"We need to find the bastard who did this and kill him," said Parks.

"Why? Because he defended himself, got the better of this miserable bunch?" Phelps stood up, stretched his back. "No. We haven't got the manpower or the means. Besides, if this individual can take out these mean assholes, including Norwich… that is no small undertaking, boys. I reckon this is one mean individual we're planning on taking down and it might be best to leave it well alone."

"I can't believe you're saying this," said Stolen. "You're supposed to be the town sheriff, for God's sake!"

"Yes, I am, and it is up to me to make difficult decisions. If we go out into the Territory, and we make mistakes, get lost or whatever, we're dead. Either from thirst, Indians, or the bastard who did this."

"But he's out there somewhere, isn't he? We'll pick up his trail easy enough because there's only one place to go, and that's Fairweather. Three days' ride. We could take our time, maybe load up a wagon, and seek him out—"

"Have you got a death-wish, Stolen, or is it just that mess of tumbleweed in your head which you like to call a brain, which makes you come out with such crap?"

"Watch your mouth, Phelps."

"Or you'll do *what,* exactly?" Phelps stuck his thumbs in his waistband. His fingers were inches away from the flintlock in his belt.

Everybody knew how good Phelps was at shooting firearms. Stolen knew it, raised a single eyebrow and snarled, "I still think we should go after him."

"Tell you what I'll do," said Phelps. "I'll give you permission, lawful, legal, call it whatever you will – damn it, I'll even sign a paper – for you and Parks to ride out and bring the bastard to justice. How about that?"

"*What*?" Parks shifted his weight, "You mean just us two?"

"You could take Rogers with you. That'll make three. Good odds, don't you think? Three-to-one?"

"You're full of shit, Phelps," said Stolen. "You haven't the guts to go out there yourself, but you're willing to send us? That stinks."

"Well, you're the ones who are so eager to track him down." He glanced towards the sky. "But if I may make one more suggestion, it would be best to leave at first light. You can't track him when the sun goes down."

"First light?" Stolen shot a glance towards Parks, who shrugged. "All right, sure, we'll do it. You sign the papers, exempt us from all wrongdoing, and we'll go get him."

Phelps grunted, took one more look at Norwich and shook his head. "You'd best be careful. I have an awful bad feeling about all of this."

* * *

Simms came into the town halfway through the following day, the horse's hooves plodding through the dirt, sending up little clouds of dust, and he pressed a bandana against his mouth and nose. The relentless heat, like a lead blanket, heavy and unbearable.

Outside the row of four buildings, which constituted the entire 'town', he tied up his sorry mount and stepped up onto the boardwalk. He dusted himself off and went through the swing doors of the saloon, this being the one building which seemed remotely alive.

The saloon was barely larger than a makeshift latrine, with three tables taking up most of the space. Two old doors, jammed together across four barrels, served as the bar. A man sat outstretched on a chair in the far corner, fast asleep. Simms rotated his shoulders, easing out the knots, and went up to the counter, rapped it with his knuckles. "Anyone home?"

The man in the corner did not stir, but through a door next to him, came the barkeeper, a leather apron spattered in blood, a filthy rag in his hands. He frowned. "Who the fuck are you?"

Simms groaned to himself. "Nice welcome. Have you got any water?"

The man snorted. "Sure. If you've got the money to pay for it."

"I've got money," said Simms. He snapped a dollar piece on the counter. "I'll need a bucket for my horse. Two canteens for myself. Three if you have another."

"That'll cost you more than a dollar, mister."

Simms sighed, looked at the floor. "Just get the goddamned water."

The barkeeper folded his arms, jaw set.

Simms put a second dollar coin next to the first. "If you ask for any more, I might get vexed."

The barkeep studied Simms from head to foot, paying particular attention to the carbine in his grip, and disappeared into the back.

From the corner, the sleeping man roused himself, blew out a loud breath and ruffled his hair with both hands. "Jeez, what time is it?"

"Past noon."

"Ah damn. Why the hell didn't anyone wake me?" He stood up and stretched, joints cracking. "I need a drink."

He waddled across to the counter and continued around it, reaching down towards a row of bottles nestling on the bottom shelf. Above was a collection of glasses, most dust-encrusted. He chose one at random, blew in it, and tipped the contents of his chosen bottle into the glass. He took a whiff of the drink's aroma, then swallowed it in one. He clung onto the shelf, head lowered, eyes squeezed shut, and gasped. "Damn, that's good." He straightened up and poured himself a second, larger drink. The bottle, now empty, he set on the counter and stumbled back to his seat. He sat and studied Simms as if noticing him for the first time. "You Baudelaire Talpas, the regulator? We been waiting on you for six weeks, you bastard. Where the hell have you been?"

"Eating cats and dogs, marrying my squaw and setting up house in Wyoming. Where the hell do you think I've been?"

The man frowned, not sure what to make of this curious retort. He decided to take a drink instead. "I reckon you ain't Talpas."

"Then you would reckon correct. I'm not a regulator."

"Bounty hunter? Jeez, you're too late for that as well! They've got the faces posted up outside what used to be the sheriff's office, before they killed him." He chuckled. "One of them bastards even added some noughts to the bounty! Would you believe that? Man, they have balls them two. Balls bigger than a buffalo's." He drank, leaned back and yawned. "My good lady is going to be so pissed. I was meant to be home by sundown. Can you imagine—"

"What was it those two boys did?"

"Waylaid poor old Mr. Shatner, the attorney. Relieved him of forty dollars, and his horse. Left him for dead out in the prairie. Rumor has it he got eaten by the coyotes."

"So how do they know these two killed poor old Mr. Shatner?"

"Because the coyotes didn't eat all of him. Sherriff found him, brought what was left of him back in town, posted the rewards, then they shot him too."

"The same boys?"

The man nodded. "Newhart and Mason. Two of the meanest sons of whores you're ever likely to find. Last I heard, they were involved in some shootout further out west, in Utah. Little town called Fairweather."

Simms held his breath. "Utah? What sort of shootout?"

"Bank robbery, so the story goes. It all went wrong, most of the gang got shot up, but them two, they managed to get away. Talk of a girl."

Simms arched a single eyebrow, stepped across the room and sat down opposite the man. He leaned forward. "A girl? What about her?"

"I don't know." The man finished his drink. "All I know is, some days later a couple of drifters showed up, full of all sorts of stories, and one of them was about Newhart and Mason. The robbery went all tits up, so some of the gang took a girl, kidnapped her. Newhart and Mason, they struck east, made their way back into Colorado. That's the last anybody knew."

"So, you have no idea where they are now?"

"No. But if you *are* a bounty-hunter, which I suspect you are, my advice would be to steer well clear of them two. They're worth not two hundred dollars between them."

The barkeeper came through the door and planted three canteens of water on the bar. He eyed the empty bottle with suspicion. "What the hell? Have you been drinking this Sandy?"

Sandy giggled, raising his glass in salutation, "Good health, Dean. I'll pay you next Friday."

"The hell you will." Dean blew out a breath and went around the bar to check the other bottles.

"Where's the bucket for my horse?"

Dean straightened, jutting his chin towards the swing doors. "I gave it to her. She's drinking it right now. She's in a sorry state, mister, and in need of a good rest. You planning on going far?"

Simms shrugged. "Colorado."

Sandy chuckled, "This here is a bounty-hunter, Dean. He's going to track down Newhart and Mason for us."

Dean pursed his lips, made a silent whistle. "Rather you than me, mister. They are mean. Shot the sheriff in the back of the head whilst he pinned up their posters. Laughed, they did. Oscar Toms went up to them, with his gun, and they shot him too. Right out there." He pointed towards the swing doors. "A lot of people left after that. Said they didn't come out west to witness that kind of devilry, and I can't say I blame 'em. I hope you're good at what you do."

"I thought he was Baudelaire."

Dean nodded. "Yes, that wouldn't be a bad guess. Are you Baudelaire, mister?"

"Not when I last checked."

"Baudelaire came here a few weeks past; said he was making his way down to Fort Laramie. Seems they're hiring men. There's a mess of trouble brewing down there. Story goes the government is sending troops."

"And not for no savages," said Sandy, leaning forward, "but for Mormons. You ever heard the like? Seems some mean types have been selling liquor to the Indians, which is against federal law, and the Mormons, they've decided to take things into their own hands."

"So I heard. My plan was to go there myself, but now…" Simms nodded. "My plans have changed somewhat. Do you know anything about this bank robbery in which Newhart and Mason were mixed up in? Something about a girl being kidnapped?"

"Only the same as Sandy here," said Dean. "Is she someone important?"

"Kind of. I've been ordered here to find her, bring her home."

Sandy shot a look between Simms and Dean. "Ordered? You mean, you ain't no bounty-hunter?"

Simms smiled at Sandy and shook his head. "No I'm not. I'm a Pinkerton Detective, out of Chicago, Illinois."

"Jesus," breathed Dean. "Then this girl truly must be awful important."

"You might say that. Now," Simms laid his hands on the table and stared. "I want you to tell me everything you know about those two jackasses, and the direction they took." He swiveled to look at Sandy. "And you too. Everything. I want to have a long conversation with 'em, if you get my meaning."

Dean levelled his attention towards Sandy, and from the expression on his face, he knew exactly what Simms meant.

* * *

Two days later, men rode into town, all of whom Dean recognized as they came clumping into his saloon, demanding beer and water.

It didn't take much of a preamble before Parks leaned across the counter and rasped, "You had a stranger in here, Dean?"

Dean, cleaning glasses with an old rag, pressed his lips together. "What's this about, Parks? Looks like you're in an awful big hurry."

"Just answer the goddamned question."

"Oh, and what are you now, the sheriff? Where is Phelps, anyway?"

"Sat on his bony ass getting drunk," spat Stolen. "Now answer, has any one passed through?"

"Had someone I thought was a bounty hunter in here. He left."

"Where'd he go?" asked Parks, taking the lead again.

"Why you interested?"

Seamus Rogers stepped up. He seemed frightened, tired, all his finer days well behind him. "Was he a tall fella, light on his feet, probably toting guns, and wearing a Derby?"

"That would be him, except he exchanged the Derby for a ten-gallon. Derbies ain't no good out in the sun, Seamus."

"We're on his trail, Dean," continued Parks. "Where did he head?"

"West, into the Territory. He's looking for someone too, but boys, I'm not sure if you should go after him. He seemed mean."

"He is. Mean as they come. He killed Norwich."

"Really?" Dean smirked. "Reckon he's done your town a favor. Norwich was a low-life and a scoundrel. You all know that."

"He stole a horse too," added Stolen, moving forward.

"Ah." Dean put down the glasses and filled them with water. "No beer, boys. Ain't had a delivery for getting on for three months. I think I've been forgotten."

"Did he say anything?"

"Only that he was after Newhart and Mason."

"Who the hell are they?"

"A pair of rattlers, the like of which I don't want ever to see again. Boys, you're going into a heap of dog-shit if you carry on after this guy. You ain't killers and you sure as hell ain't trackers. You'll get lost and end up dying of thirst out there. Best leave it, go back home."

"I think he's right," said Rogers, head bobbing as if he no longer had neck muscles.

"Shut your face," spat Stolen. "That miserly sonofabitch killed Norwich. I don't give a rat's ass who or what Norwich was, but he was a member of our town, and if we let this go, what does that say about us, eh?"

"It says you're wise, Stolen. You know your limitations. Ain't no shame in that. Leave 'em all to the elements, or to the Indians. One of them will end everything for 'em, that's for sure."

"This is bullshit," snapped Parks. "Where *exactly* west did he go?"

"Mentioned Fort Laramie, but maybe Fort Bridger first. There's a heap of trouble that way, boys. Everywhere you look, it's the same. Death is the only thing waiting for you if you continue on this venture, so let it go."

"You're an old woman, Dean," snarled Parks.

"At least I'm a live one."

He pushed over the filled glasses. Leaned back and watched them drink. He didn't think he'd ever see them again, so he refrained from informing them exactly who Simms was. The detective might tell them himself, before he killed them.

Five

The ranch house was a solid-looking building on two levels, wooden fascia painted gleaming white, the roof made from neat, black slate. A covered porch, surrounded by a fence, with a gate and steps, had various chairs and tables arranged across, and adjacent to the main door, paintings and cleaning implements rested upon the wall.

Newhart pull on the reins and the wagon stopped. He whistled. "This must have cost a tidy sum," he said, leaning forward on the buckboard to peer out from under the brim of his hat. He hawked and spat into the dirt. "Mason, I think we got something here."

After a moment, Mason poked his head through the flap of the wagon. He was naked, but without shame, he slipped up beside Newhart and grinned. "Oh my, that looks a fine place."

"It seems new."

"Maybe it is."

"Why would anyone build such a thing all the way out here?"

"Maybe they found God."

"Hardly likely." Newhart rubbed his chin. "You think there'll be working men around here?"

"I'd take a bet on it. So, we need to be real careful."

"What you planning on doing, Mason?"

"Take it for our own, of course. We go up nice and easy, you and the girl together up front, making out as if you're settlers or something. I'll wait inside the wagon, and when they're not watching, slip out 'round the back of the building back and plug any bastards slinking around. Then we'll hole up, maybe for a few days. They must have plenty of supplies, maybe a good woman to help with the cooking."

"Jesus, all you ever think about is women. Ain't you got enough with the girl back there?"

"She is a sweet young thing. She told me she's nineteen. *Nineteen.* She's as smooth as beaver-skin, Newhart, her body lean, so giving."

Newhart rubbed his face. "I don't need the details of how much she excites you, I hear you often enough. Every goddamned minute, night and day."

"She loves it. Didn't at first, but now..." He chuckled and looked down at his growing arousal. "I'm in heaven, Newhart. I can't get enough."

Newhart stared at his friend's impressive erection, licked his lips. "God, Mason, you are something, I have to say."

Mason chuckled again, patted Newhart's shoulder and said, "Give me a minute or two, then I'll send her up front." Then he disappeared into the interior. Within seconds, the wagon rocked gently from side to side, moans filling the air.

Newhart sighed, flicked the horse with the reins and the wagon lurched forward, creaking and groaning across the pitted, hard-backed land.

* * *

Stockport Lancing sat by the window, peering out between the drapes, focusing on the approaching wagon. Beside him was his old army rifle, a single-shot flintlock. Ranger, his old dog, stretched and yawned, a low grumble coming from the back of his throat.

"You stay quiet now, boy," said Lancing. Behind him, Joanna, his maid, played with a towel, wrapping and re-wrapping it around her fists.

"Should I nip out back and fetch the boys," she asked.

"Maybe. Give it a second or two. Looks like a couple, and I can't see no firearms. Maybe they are settlers, lost their way."

"We haven't had any visitors here for almost a year. It's hard to miss the trail nowadays. They ain't lost, Mr. Lancing, sir."

He nodded, knowing the truth of her words. Since the gold rush, the trail was as good as signposted all the way along. No one came this way anymore, unless they were sick or dying. Or here to steal. "Fetch the boys," he said. "And take Ranger outside, I don't want him barking."

She did so, leading the old dog by the collar towards the rear door.

Lancing frowned. "Now, I wonder what the hell you want?"

* * *

Newhart shifted his weight. Thc buckboard was harder than iron, causing his backside to become numb. He fought back the desire to jump down and give his buttocks a well-deserved massage.

Elisabeth, sitting beside him, noticed his discomfort and laughed. "You got lice in your pants?"

He sniggered. "I got them everywhere, little girl. No, it's my ass. I can't hardly feel it."

"Well, maybe when we get inside you could take a bath." She sniffed the air. "You need one."

"You have a tongue on you, little girl, I'll say that much. Doesn't Mason stink bad too?"

"No. Mason smells divine."

"You like him, don't you?"

"Some." She gave a short laugh. "Does that make you jealous?"

He snapped his head around to face her and for a moment he wanted to tell her exactly what he thought of her, but then his eyes fell on her smooth, full lips and he melted. "Christ, yes."

"Thought so." She smiled. "Best not let Mason hear you saying such a thing. He's like to slit your throat."

"That would be the truth, but hell… You two moving around like two rabbits, it's driving me crazy."

"Well, you just keep a lid on it because Mason and me..." She sighed then looked out across the rolling land to the house. "That's a nice place. Wonder how they manage to keep it so clean. Can't be a working place."

Newhart shrugged. He had to agree. The building was pristine, virtually glowing in the sunshine. The perfect paintwork, gleaming windows, and roof as shiny as if it were a polished mirror, all seemed to point to the building as newly-built. Two stories, with three windows in the roof and a chimney stack on either end. This was a large house, and the closer Newhart took the wagon, the more impressive it seemed. A set of steps led up to the front porch, an oil lamp swinging from the rafters by a hook. Two rocking chairs, a low table and cushions waited under the awning. A perfect place to while away the long evenings. "I think it's some sort of retirement place," said Newhart, easing the wagon to the left and setting it before a nearby hitching rail. "This ain't no cattle ranch."

"A hotel maybe?"

"All the way out here? Nah. Let's go and take a look." He jumped down, dusted off his coat, put his palms into the small of his back, and stretched himself.

"Help me down, Newhart."

He grinned, bowed with exaggerated sarcasm, and held out his hand. She gripped it and jumped onto the hard ground. She looked around, then concentrated on the upper story. "I think there's someone watching."

"Well, let's hope they're friendly."

"You think they have big beds? Soft mattresses, thick blankets?"

"Why, you fixing on sleeping the rest of the day?"

"No," she said, smiling, "I'm thinking of curling up next to Mason under real cotton sheets is what I'm thinking."

"Jeez girl, you're as bad as he is! All you think about is—"

The main door creaked open and an elderly man stepped out onto the porch, holding a long musket in his hands. He studied them both for a moment. "I'll be asking you who you are, friends, and what you're doing on my property?"

"We left the trail a while back," said Elisabeth quickly, before Newhart could get a word out. She stepped forward, spreading out her hands, "thinking we might find a short-cut. Instead, all we found was prairie. Until we saw this place."

"It's mighty fine," breathed Newhart, stepping up next to Elisabeth, resting his hand on her slim shoulder. "Me and my sister, we're heading out west. Lost Ma and Pa on the way…"

Elisabeth shrugged him off and took another step towards the old man, making it to the bottom step before he levelled the musket directly at her. "We just need some water, maybe a little food. A while to rest. Our horse, he's mighty tired, as you can see."

"Yes, I can see." The old man's eyes never left hers. A tiny frown appeared on his brow. "Are you all right? I mean, not just from being exposed to the weather and all, I mean, are you *all right*?"

She smiled, mounting the first step and her eyes closed, as she mouthed a silent 'no'. She stopped, two steps from the top. "Are you all alone out here?"

"No I ain't."

"Elisabeth," breathed Newhart, his voice dangerous, edged with ice, low, "what the good fuck are you doing?"

Elisabeth, ignoring Newhart's sense of panic and the atmosphere charging with tension, took another step, gaze set solid on the old man. "Get everyone you can out here with a gun and," she grinned, "shoot these bastards to Kingdom come!"

Newhart yelped as Elisabeth launched herself forward, tore the musket from the old man's gnarled fingers, turned and fired.

Newhart flung himself to the ground, the musket ball whizzing mere inches over his head, and he rolled underneath the wagon, fumbling for his revolver in the folds of his coat.

"Get inside," shrieked Elisabeth, pushing the old man through the open door with such force he toppled over backwards. She kicked the door shut with the sole of her boot and dropped to her knees as Newhart's first bullet smashed through the woodwork and pinged through the room.

She didn't have time to take in her surroundings, but she was aware of the size of the room, its coolness, the shutters closed to keep out the sun's heat. The old man whimpered and three people appeared from a back room, a woman and two men. They were young, early twenties, and were all armed.

"Shoot them," she snarled.

"Them?"

"There's two. The bastard under the wagon and another, much worse. He's already skirting 'round back."

"Who the hell are you?"

"Don't argue, just shoot them!"

Another bullet smashed through the woodwork, cutting off her speech and the two men moved, fanning out to the windows either side of the main door. The woman was mumbling, wringing her hands. "Oh, sweet Jesus."

And that was when Mason came through from the back and into the room, a gun in each hand.

Six

From his vantage point, Simms watched their progress through a pair of army-issue binoculars and waited, his breathing low and easy. Nevertheless, he felt disappointed. He had hoped against hope the posse would never have managed to come to fruition. Of course, if he thought about it hard enough, he knew, deep down, they had to come. They would have laughed at his note, probably shared the payment between themselves, and decided on killing him regardless. His chief surprise, however, lay in their ability to track him. Or maybe it was simple luck. There were few routes west towards Bridger, they just happened to have picked the right one.

He checked his carbine and squinted down the barrel. There were three of them. Another few minutes, there would be two. The others might then give it up and retreat to their homes and loved ones. He hoped so. Killing was his trade, but he was meant to be an investigator, not an assassin. What was it Sandy called him, a *regulator*? He'd heard the term before, used for hired gunmen to help in disputes, range wars, all sorts of troubles between individuals or groups as the Territories expanded west at the end of the Mexican War. Some of these disagreements would result in a much wider conflict, he felt sure, but he hoped this was still some years away. He needed to turn his back on this business, find someone to settle down with, enjoy what remained of his life. Money, or the lack of it, was the problem, and a good enough reason to hunt Newhart and Mason down. Not just for the good general's sake, but for his own. Two hundred dollars would serve well, allow him to put down a grubstake, build a place. Farm.

He spat into the dirt, and wiped the sweat from his eyebrow with the back of his hand. Farm. What did he know about farming? He'd never so much as picked up a shovel, except to bury his comrades in arms. That was not what farming was about. He'd need to read a book, study, perhaps set up with someone who knew what they were doing. A woman would be good, but how many single women were there out here in this hellhole? Women who were not as thick-set as a grizzled gold-miner, whose hands were not calloused, whose bodies were slim, yielding. He closed his mind for a moment allowing the fantasy to develop, of him with a young, slim blonde, living a life under an empty sky, with a warm bed waiting at the end of the day.

"Shit," he said, snapping open his eyes to find his quarry out of sight, slipping behind a large, imposing boulder. He would have to wait until they emerged on the other side. His hillside vantage point was strewn with rocks and scrub and the approach afforded any would-be attacker fine cover. He'd need to wait, until they were close enough for him to bring the Dragoon to bear. The carbine was an excellent weapon, but if he missed… He should have taken another rifle from Norwich's store, damn his fat hide. And more cartridges too.

He stretched his legs, lowered the carbine, and waited.

* * *

"I don't think I can take much more of this," said Rogers, draped over the neck of his horse. "We need water. Rest. Maybe we should turn back."

"Quit your moaning," growled Parks. "All you've done since the moment we left town is moan, moan, fucking moan! Ride on back if you want to, but I'm not stopping until that bastard is tethered across the back of his horse, dead."

"He has a point though," said Stolen, as they moved into the shade of a massive outcrop of rock. He reined in his horse, took out his canteen and shook it. "I ain't got more than a drop or two left to drink, Parks. Let's stay here for a while, out of the sun. We're pushing too damned hard."

Parks stopped, bowed his head. He needed to admit it, they were lost, out of water and if they didn't come across a homestead or town soon, they'd die out here. Just like Dean told them. He twisted in his saddle. "You think we should go back too?"

"It's a consideration. I believe we took the wrong trail. I reckon he went south, not south west. We should have picked him up by now."

"We can't go back," said Parks. "We're too far gone. We'd never make it."

Stolen blew out his breath. "Well shit, Parks, then I say we camp here, get us some rest, then start out again tomorrow."

"Or later tonight," said Rogers. "It would be better travelling at night. Out of the sun. We'd not sweat as much, not need as much water. Let's rest here until the sun goes down, then continue."

Parks nodded. "That's the most sense you've made since you were born, I reckon." He squinted skywards. "Beats me why it doesn't rain. How long has it been now, a month? Six weeks? Feels like forever. Anyways, this is a good spot. If that bastard is around here, it might be better to move through these hills in the dark. He might even be watching us now."

"You think so?" Rogers, bolt upright, edged towards the far end of the boulder and peeped out. He turned his feverish gaze to the top of the hill, but immediately turned away, dazzled by the sun, which hung low in the sky behind the crest. "Holy Mother, I can't get a good enough look – what if he is there, waiting?"

"All the more reason to sit," said Stolen and eased himself out of his saddle. He patted his horse and set about hobbling it.

Rogers watched him and chewed away at his bottom lip. "Okay, let's wait here, Parks, yeah? You agree?"

"I agree," said Parks. "This trail leads all the way down to Bridger. If that is where he's heading, that is where we'll find him. Whether today, tomorrow or next week, it doesn't much matter, I guess. His days are numbered, that I swear."

* * *

Simms lay waiting amongst the rocks for a long time, growing more restless, thinking perhaps they'd double-backed, flanked him, were about to come pouring down the hillside behind him. He needed to act, to flush them out, bring the fight to them. He rolled over, squeezing fingers into his eyes. He took a mouthful of water from his canteen, checked his carbine again and set off, bent double, skirting around the large rocky outcrop to his left. Constantly checking the rock, he scrambled across a mound of shale, feet slipping out from under him, and got down amongst some bushes. The thorns and knotted twigs bit into the exposed flesh of his hands and cheeks. He winced, but kept any sound to a minimum. He measured his breathing and slithered across the remaining distance like a snake, eyes ahead, belly stabbed and jabbed by the stony ground.

He saw them, flattened himself. They were perhaps twenty paces ahead, the thin aged guy closest, back to the giant boulder, asleep. The other two were digging a small pit in the rocky ground. This might be an attempt to fashion a sort of natural cooking oven, but Simms wasn't sure. He'd seen Indians in Mexico doing something similar, slow cooking prairie dogs or buck rabbits over hot stones, the pit covered with bracken and leaves. But there were no leaves here. A lot of bracken, mind you, so maybe this was a variation on a theme. Perhaps he should try it.

One of the men, with his back to him, stood up and pulled off his coat. He threw it to the ground and stretched out his limbs.

Simms rose up from his cover like the dark avenger, and shot the man between the shoulder blades with the carbine. He immediately raced forward, covering the twenty or so paces at a charge, dropping the carbine, exchanging it for the Colt Dragoon.

The remaining man by the pit fumbled for his own gun, managed to get it out before Simms put three bullets into him and dumped him on his back.

The old wizened guy was screaming, standing with his fists in his mouth. Simms sauntered up to him and put the muzzle of his gun against the man's temple. "Do you remember me?" The old man shook his head, body quivering. Simms glared. "You sent me over to your friend, Norwich. Well, you won't be doing that again, you son of a bitch."

"Oh, sweet Jesus," moaned the old guy, emptying his bladder and sphincter in one. The stench rose up and Simms tottered backwards. "Oh sweet Jesus!"

Simms gagged, turning away, covering his mouth. The man he'd previously shot in the back groaned, giving Simms an excuse to move further downwind of the smell.

He prodded the stricken man with the toe of his boot. The man moaned again, and Simms put his foot under the man's ribcage and hauled him over onto his back.

"You heartless bastard," the man managed.

Across the scree, the old man moved. It may have been an attempt to escape, or more likely make a wild grab for a gun. Either way, Simms was past caring. He swung, crouched low, fanned the hammer of his Dragoon and sent two heavy slugs into the man's body, blowing him apart. He put the last bullet through the head of the man on the ground.

The boom of the shots echoed across the prairie, signaling the gruesome event to anyone within a few miles. Soon the buzzards would circle. When Simms moved on, they would feast on the exposed bodies of the dead, all remaining evidence to the killing gone forever. He liked that and took in a deep breath.

Simms took a few careful moments to reload his Dragoon, clearing out each cylinder before priming them with powder, ball and cap. He then moved over to the horses. Hobbled, they couldn't run off, but they were well spooked. It took him some time to calm them before he checked saddlebags, searching for ammunition. He found none. Relief came when he discovered half a canteen of water. He took a mouthful, found it tainted but swallowed it anyway. Out here, in this stricken land, decisions were simple. Water, any water, was the most precious commodity of all. There were no choices.

He unburdened the horses of their saddles. He kept the best of the animals, let the other two run free and he stood and watched them gallop off across the prairie, great clouds of dust in their wake.

He sat in the shade of the boulder, the flies already settling on the wounds of the dead. Simms watched them for a long time before he leaned back against the rock, tipped his hat over his eyes and slept, the first occasion for some time he'd rested without fear of attack.

Seven

The room clung with the stink of cordite, the walls continuing to resound with the blasts from the many discharged firearms. Elisabeth crouched behind an ancient piano, an instrument that would never again ring out its plaintive tones. Two bullets had ripped through its sides, shattering hammers, destroying ivory. The girl huddled herself into the corner, trembling, wondering what would happen next.

From where she sat, she could see the body of the old man, lying spread-eagled across the floor, his eyes wide open, the back of his head nothing more than a gaping, black hole. The sadness threatened to overwhelm her. She didn't know the old man, but something about him reminded her of her father, and she imagined General Randall in a similar position, the life seeping out from the wounds in his shattered body. They should never have come to this hostile land, with its many dangers and uncertainties. Father had convinced her a new life, full of promise, awaited them in the unchartered plains of the Territories. They'd set off, so full of optimism, but as soon as they left Missouri and crossed the endless expanse of nothing, their hearts sank as the realization of their situation struck home. This was no land flowing with milk and honey; it was hard and harsh, unremitting and unforgiving. She sobbed when she remembered their life back in Chicago, their house, neighbors and friends, the normality of it all. And now this, sheltering from a maniac whose only thoughts were of death, the killing of innocents, the taking of possessions. Mason. She hated him with every fiber of her being and longed to see him dead.

She recalled the dreadful moment everything changed. The day of the bank robbery, they dragged her around the corner, shooting their guns, and she left her father on the boardwalk, dying. She fought, kicking, scratching, but to no avail. The larger of the two men, whose name she soon discovered was Mason, struck her across the mouth and the resistance left her. Half-dazed, she recalled little of the next few moments, save for the constant bucking and jostling of the wagon, the constant gunfire, the screams of indignation, fear, sorrow.

When at last they stopped, Mason took advantage of her, his rough hands all over her body, his stinking breath close to her ear, the pounding of his loins. Afterwards, she vomited, self-loathing overcoming her. He seemed not to care. He visited her constantly, his member a brutal, rigid club, forever ramming, no gentleness, never any thought for her. She screamed those first dozen times, unable to accommodate him without experiencing the most awful splitting sensation. Walking proved difficult, so she took to lying in the tent, shivering naked under the blankets until he would come to her again, pull the covers away, and drive into her without a pause until he was spent. She learned if she moaned rather than screamed, he would become more gentle; if she caressed his shoulders, ran her hand through his hair, he would raise himself up, his thrusts less violent, and if she cooed and moaned, 'Yes, like that, just like that', it may take longer but it was so much less painful. Sometimes she would lie beside him and run her hands over him and he would cry out like a baby and she understood the power she had, the control. After numerous couplings, she allowed him to kiss her, and he was gentle, giving, more in tune with her needs. She scolded herself the night her own fire swept across her loins, recalling how his tongue sought out her most private places. She curled up next to him, ashamed and all the angrier for it. She did not show then, before or since, the hatred, which dwelled inside. She decided to enjoy what she could, to be selfish, and wait. Wait for the moment when he became so infatuated, so convinced she was his, that his guard would drop and she would strike. For she hated him and whenever he went off to scan the horizon, she would vomit in the dirt. And when he returned, she would smile, throw back the blanket and gesture for him to enter her once again.

Huddling there behind the broken piano, trembling with fear and self-loathing, the truth surfaced.

The hatred she bore for herself was greater than what she felt for him.

And now, here she was, so close to seeing him die. But he hadn't died. The man was blessed, in some perverse way. He stood in the doorway, his bulk silhouetted against the sunlight, six-gun smoking in his hand, contemptuous of danger, dismissive of death.

The two young men sheltered behind upturned pieces of furniture. One desperately reloaded his musket whilst the second covered him with his own six-gun, rising every so often to fire two or three shots towards the door. Not one bullet struck home and Mason laughed. "You better run, you fuckers, for I'm gonna skin you when this is done. You hear me, skin you alive!"

Elisabeth knew it to be so. On the journey over, they came across a couple, the axle of their wagon broken. The woman, plump, grim-faced, swathed in a padded, dark blue dress, busied herself setting up a lean to, draping a tarpaulin over the top as a sort of makeshift roof. Newhart pulled up their horse and leaned forward.

"You folks in trouble?"

"Bust an axle on this rocky ground," said the man. "You'd best be wary yourself, friend. The ground is like iron, no moisture in it."

Newhart nodded, looking around. "You come across any riders?"

"Indians, you mean?"

"No. Just riders."

"Desperadoes?" bleated the woman, standing motionless, playing with the hem of her dress. "Oh sweet Jesus, are they killers, robbers?"

"Just about everything bad you can put a label to roams across this prairie, ma'am."

"Oh, my sweet Jesus," she said and ran up to her man, throwing her arms around his waist. "Can we not join you?"

"Four is better than two," said the man. "We had to kill our horse, but we still have some of the meat. We have grain, too, flour, beans. Water."

"Ah," smiled Newhart. "Water is like gold around these parts."

"We have some gold too," said the woman and her man shot her a terrified look.

Too late for life to continue.

Mason came around the back of the wagon and shot the man through the throat. The woman screamed and he cuffed her across the face with his gun. She fell down, nose and mouth smashed, the blood leaking from broken teeth and bone. He straddled her. Elisabeth, watching from her place next to Newhart, screamed in disgust and Mason jerked his head around. "I'm not violating her, sweet darlin', so have no fear of that." He slipped out the heavy-bladed Bowie from inside his coat and sliced off her nose. She writhed, her blood-curdling cries shrieking across the plains. Mason stood, studied the man on the ground, clutching at his throat, thrashing his legs, desperate to stop his life draining through his fingers. "Poor bastard," said Mason and went over to the broken wagon and sifted through their belongings. Anything of use he took. He grinned at Newhart, who laughed. Mason clambered into the back and fell asleep, snoring like a mule. They continued, rattling across the stony ground and Elisabeth craned her neck to look back at the couple; the woman, blood cascading down her destroyed face, cradling her dead man's body, wailing. Already the buzzards were circling overhead. Elizabeth said a silent prayer, but knew it would do no good. This land was cursed.

Much later, when Elisabeth dared to ask him why he had left the woman so disfigured, Mason shrugged. "People need to learn lessons."

"*Lessons*? What the hell do you mean by that, Mason?"

"People come out here believing it to be some sort of tea-party, that all they have to do is load up their wagon and spend a few days travelling forever west and salvation, peace and glory awaits. Well, it ain't so. Look at you, a father dead, your future nothing like what you planned. This is a hard land, darlin', and I am its prophet of doom."

"So you disfigured her so that others might see the error of their ways?"

"I did indeed. I am a man of simple beliefs, darlin', and one who knows his place on this good Earth. My duty is to save all those who would dare come into this land without full understanding of its cruelties."

"You truly are a savior," she said, snuggling into him, her arm snaking around his waist, her other dropping to his groin. "I think I love you, Mason."

"I know you do, darlin'," he said, smoothing her hair, "I know you do."

If he knew the truth, he would have killed her there and then.

From behind the piano, she saw the maid, slumped in the corner, her chest barely moving. A bullet had smashed her left shoulder, but she was tough. Her head came up and their eyes locked. A thin snarl of a smile. With a grimace, she managed to reach behind her, pulling out a revolver. She nodded and Elisabeth returned the gesture. The maid pushed it across the floor with all of her remaining strength before Mason shot her in the head.

Elisabeth bit back a mixed cry of frustration and horror. These people lived out a good, clean existence, never intending any harm to man nor beast. Newhart and Mason changed all of that. Damn their eyes. She saw the gun, lying there within five paces, so tempting. Perhaps she could make a grab for it, perhaps she might succeed. Perhaps. But far more certainly, Mason would shoot her before she got within an arm's length. Despite all of his amorous intentions, he would not falter when it came to killing her. The man was a demon. Life, and its continuance, was not something he considered important. Not the lives of others, that is. He believed himself blessed, never more so in how arrogantly he stood in the doorway, dismissive of danger, waiting.

"Come on out Elisabeth," he growled. "Don't you worry none, darlin', I won't hurt you. Not too much any ways. What I'll do first is, I'll make love to you all night long, and you know there is nothing finer in this world than how I make you feel. Then, when you are spent, I might just tickle that fine rump of yours with my belt for you know you need a good scolding. So come on out, sweet darlin' and join your loving daddy."

She caught the bewildered look of one of the young men, who having completed the reloading of his musket, was mouthing something to her. But she could not catch any of it, so she shrugged, shook her head, and pointed to the gun, miming the firing of the musket. Perhaps he understood, perhaps not. So she mimed it all again, jerking her thumb towards her chest, firing the pistol with her fingers, urging him with her wide, bright eyes to shoot with his own weapon.

She blew out her breath and sank back against the wall. It was hopeless, he didn't understand. Soon Mason would come striding closer and he'd kill them all. She gave up a silent prayer and closed her eyes.

The main door blasted open and Newhart came in, coat tails wrapping around his legs. A sudden squall accompanied his dramatic entrance, sending everyone into a whirlwind of confusion, including Mason who swung around towards his friend. Elisabeth took her chance and went for the gun. She needed to calculate who to shoot. Given all that had happened, a casual observer might have reasoned she would choose Mason. After all, he was the one who abused her, relentlessly. But something stopped Elisabeth from this course, something she could never fully understand. Perhaps it was the man's almost mystical invincibility, perhaps she simply did not have the strength or courage to kill. Whatever the reason, she turned the gun on Newhart and shot him in the thigh. He yelped and staggered backwards, stumbling over the steps.

Mason let out a long wail and raced towards his stricken friend. Meanwhile, the two young men were on their knees, aiming down the lengths of their muskets. They discharged their firearms at the same time, but not one shot hit their assailant and the last Elisabeth saw of Mason was that demonic look in his eyes as he glared back at her. In that lingering glance she saw replayed all that had passed between them over the previous endless, relentless days. If ever he harbored any feelings for her from those times, nothing registered in his face. He turned away, lifted Newhart in his great arms with ease and carried him towards their waiting wagon. Elisabeth dragged herself to her feet and loosed off five shots at his retreating frame. Every one missed, but at least the fusillade quickened his flight and he broke into a tottering run. She followed him and stood in the doorway, watching him place Newhart in the back, climb up onto the buckboard seat and flick the reins. She watched him rumble off into the distance and she didn't stop watching until he was nothing but a smudge on the horizon. A strange calmness settled over her, overwhelming relief and gladness at his departure. And happiness too, for the next she would learn of him would be news of his death. She smiled at the thought.

Eight

The tented village sprawled across the land in ordered rows, white canvas sparkling like new fallen spots of snow. He wished it was snow, for then he might find something to drink. To reinforce his despair, he lifted his final canteen to his ear and shook it. Empty. Perhaps some kind soul below would allow him a mouthful of water. Down in the camp. Down in the gathering of armed men settling around Fort Bridger.

Simms entered the camp at a measured pace, leading his horse, trying his best to ignore the many upturned faces of the curious soldiers. Guards stopped him, and when he presented his papers, they waved him on, bored, apathetic. They appeared drained, the heat making every movement an effort.

He tended to his horse first, as every good traveler should. A trough, hewn out of a split log, stood in the center of the encampment and two men in uniforms obscured by layers of grey dust, nodded when he asked. After the horse put its nose into the trough, the desperation overcame him and he threw back his hat and plunged his face into the warm water beside his animal, splashing his face, hair, neck. It felt like the most glorious thing he had ever experienced.

Nearby soldiers laughed, but Simms didn't care. He raised his head, eyes closed, water dripping down onto his chest, basking in the sensation as the liquid cooled his flesh, brought life back to his limbs.

"You come a long way, mister?"

Simms blinked, running a hand over his face, and forced a small smile. "Farther than I care to think about."

The soldiers exchanged a look. "It can't have been easy, crossing the range. We got food too if you're hungry, over at the canteen. It'll cost you, though."

"I've got money."

"Well that's something, at least. Not many drifters have."

"I'm not a drifter."

"No," said the other, burlier of the two, "I can see that."

"You a bounty hunter?"

"Lawman."

Both soldiers gaped at that. The burly one recovered first. "Well, if you're here to arrest the Mormons, you'd best be quick about it. We're going to kick ass right soon."

"It's not Mormons I'm after. A kidnapped girl, daughter of a retired general in the Federal Army. A man of some distinction. The girl was taken by two desperadoes, so I need to speak to your commanding officer and learn what he might know."

"Well," the smaller one scratched the side of his nose, "not sure he'd be of a mind to talk to you, given all the plans and preparations he's a-making. He's not the most amiable of gentlemen, it has to be said. Best find yourself somewhere to rest up until this hullaballoo is settled."

"And when might that be?"

Another exchange of looks. The burly one shrugged. "When they're all dead."

"Who?"

"The Mormons. That's why we're here, mister, to bring law and order to the Territories and teach those righteous bastards a lesson they won't forget."

Simms's breath trailed between his lips. Nothing he saw or heard so far filled him with confidence at finding Elisabeth Randall, or the two men who took her. Previous warnings about what was occurring around Bridger prepared him for the sea of trouble he was entering into, but even so, the reality concerned him.

He narrowed his eyes as he looked beyond the rows of tents, to where Fort Bridger had once stood, its cluster of buildings now charred, burned out shells. Men crawled like ants across the blackened remains, removing timber, clearing the area. "What is it they've done, exactly?"

The smaller one hawked and spat into the dirt. "Enough. They burned down the old fort, that was one thing. Lucky no one died."

"I've heard it said someone was selling liquor to the natives. That's against federal law."

"Law don't count for much out here. Besides, them Mormons, they want the right to make their own laws, to live the way they want to live. Government don't like that, no sir-ree. Either way, the reasons we're here don't much matter."

"I guess they might to the Mormons."

"Well, the talking is done, mister." He frowned. "You ain't one of them is you?"

"I'm as God-fearing as the next man," Simms winked, "even you, private, but I ain't no Mormon."

"A marshal, is that what you is?"

"Kind of. A detective. From Chicago. I'm here to find the General's girl like I said, and I really do need to speak with your commander."

The soldiers both shrugged and, after some dithering, led him between the neat rows of tents, past surly looking soldiers who glowered and snarled, towards a group of three larger tents, the main one in the center sprouting a Union Flag and guarded by two soldiers bearing rifles. The burly soldier spoke to one of the guards who, after shooting Simms a dark look, dipped inside. After a moment, he returned and gestured Simms to enter.

The smaller one touched his arm. "You be careful, mister. Colonel Johnston don't take kindly to strangers."

Simms nodded his thanks and went inside.

Three officers, one crouched over a large map, gathered around a feeble-looking trestle table. The one in the center, thinning hair swept over his pate, looked out from under heavy, threatening brows, weasel eyes narrowed, uncompromising.

"You're a detective?" he growled. Simms nodded. "What sort of damned detective might you be?"

Simms reached inside his coat and pulled out his threadbare wallet, the one he always kept close to his heart. He opened it and turned it towards the assembled officers. Inside was his badge, and personal details. All the army officers squinted. "Pinkerton. My name is Simms. I'm on the trail of two desperadoes who kidnapped the daughter of General Randall, former expedition leader in the Mexican War, under whom I served with great pride and devotion."

Johnston held up his hand. "I don't want no sermon, boy. Just tell me what it is you want. You may have noticed, but we're up to our necks in shit right now, so if it's help you're seeking, we ain't got it."

Simms pressed his lips together and slipped his wallet inside his coat. "I want information, Colonel, nothing more. These two men are loathsome, murdering sons of bitches. It is my job to bring them to justice and save the girl."

"If they're as bad as you say," interjected the officer crouched over the map, "why don't you simply kill 'em?"

"I may well have to, sir."

"Then gets to doing it," the officer continued. He straightened himself, wincing with the effort. "We've been here for weeks, getting ourselves ready for an expedition into the heart of Mormon territory. It's a wild, empty space where people simply get gobbled up. They disappear. We sent two groups of messengers out across the dirt, and neither have been seen or heard of since. I doubt if the ones you seek are still alive. However, there is a place, a ranch, the only one for miles. They are Mormons, but have not involved themselves with the hostilities and they have made some sort of pact with the natives, so they are free from most dangers."

"Where is all this leading, Calhoon?" demanded Johnston.

"There might be an outside chance the men you seek went there, so it's worth a try. However, it's a dangerous trek. I'll give you men, and you can track those varmints down, even kill them if you've a mind to. But before you do, you might want to consider a little proposition I might have for you."

Johnston's fierce gaze blazed with greater intensity. "What the hell are you talking about, Calhoon? What proposition?"

"We need a message delivered to Lieutenant Ives on the steamboat 'Explorer'. As I said, we've already tried to send him two, but with no success. You make sure the note gets to him, Detective and you can have a platoon to help you bring in your quarry."

"And what makes you think I can succeed where your others have not?"

Calhoon shrugged. He slowly took a fat cigar from the top pocket of his uniform jacket, bit off the end and spat it into the dust. "I've heard about you Pinkertons. You're resourceful, clever. You're also not frightened to use a gun." He pointed to the carbine in Simms's grip. "I reckon you fit the bill, mister. You've already crossed the wilderness, so you must be tough. Tougher than the greenhorns we have here, for sure. You deliver this note; we help you get your men."

Johnston blew out his cheeks. "That's a fine proposition, Lieutenant Calhoon. It might just work, too. What do you say, mister?"

"The name is Simms. Detective Simms."

"Well, all righty, *Detective*, what do you say to this proposal?"

Simms rubbed his chin. "I'm thinking I could find this isolated ranch myself."

"I'm thinking I might just throw you into a hole, in chains," said Johnston. "For all we know, you might be a Mormon infiltrator. Make your mind up."

Simms did, in less than two heartbeats. "Seems I have little choice."

"Choice has got nothing to do with it," growled Johnston. "We're here to get a job done, just like you. We're all on the same side, Detective, but just for now, I'm the one giving the orders."

"When do you want me to leave?"

"As soon as you've cleaned up. Get yourself some food, Detective, restore your strength. You're gonna need it."

Simms believed the Colonel's words were, unfortunately, true.

Nine

Outside one of the many tents, Simms managed to reunite with the two soldiers who first greeted him on his arrival into the camp. They appeared amused when he told them he was now working for the Federal Army.

"And you were drafted?" asked the smaller of the two.

"You could say that." He put out his hand. "My name is Simms, I'm a law officer out of Chicago, Illinois."

"Harvey Winterton," said the smaller, "out of Missouri. This here is Felix Ableman, also out of Missouri." The big, gruff soldier squeezed out a smile from between his heavy jowls. "What's a law officer gonna do for us?"

Simms shrugged and glanced around the throng of serried tents, men of all shapes and sizes, cleaning weapons, singing songs, repairing uniforms. Most seemed cheerful enough, nothing like how it was back in the Mexican War, when he spent every day in a puddle of his own urine, wondering where the next bullet was coming from. "What are these boys gonna do?"

"Well, news is," said Winterton, leaning forward, "not a whole lot."

"I don't get it."

"This ain't no *war*, it's just the government flexing its muscles. It's pissed that Brigham Young is asserting his independence, not towing the line, all that bull. Rumor has it none of us will ever get to fire our shiny new rifles, that all we'll have to do is march west and them Mormons will simply give it all up."

"Let's hope the rumors are true."

"Sounds like you know a lot about it," put in Ableman, his stare penetrating, as if he were waiting to notice the slightest flicker of a lie.

"Some," said Simms, stretching his legs. "I fought in the Mexican War, got a medal."

"A medal? Jesus," said Winterton. "You mean, for bravery and such?"

Simms nodded. "It's not something I tend to talk about."

"And why is that?" Ableman said, his voice hard-edged, forever probing.

Simms held the man's gaze. "Killing ain't easy, friend. I learned pretty quick to close my mind to it. Since then, it's stayed closed. War does that. Strips away your decency, makes you numb to the suffering you inflict."

"But they were your enemies."

"They were human beings." Simms turned away, growing uncomfortable at the man's words, his manner. "I'm here to do a job, a very simple job, and once it's done your good Colonel is going to give me some men to help me locate the girl I'm after." He chuckled, and swung his head around to face Ableman again. "Who knows, it might even be you."

Ableman hawked and spat and they all watched the frothy blob disappear into the parched ground. "When this is over, I'm going back to my work in my hometown. I'm a carpenter, making doors, tables, carts."

"A noble profession."

"Better than being a killer."

Simms nodded. "Can't argue with you there. What about you?" He looked across at Winterton.

"Tailor. Well," he grinned, "apprentice to a tailor, to be more accurate."

"Seems to me you boys shouldn't even be here."

Winterton agreed, "We were visited by a recruiting party, set up on a stage in the town square, rattling drums, showing us the fancy uniforms. Told us we could sign up for two years, make some money to send home to our families."

"Told us we wouldn't even have to fight, that there was no danger." Ableman shook his great head. "That was the first lie they told."

"The second was the one about the money." Winterton scratched a pattern in the dust with the toe of his boot. "We ain't barely been paid more than a few dollars. They keep telling us we'll get all we're due, but I reckon they hope we'll get ourselves shot before they have to pay up."

"Thought you said the rumor was there'd be no fighting?"

"Yes, that's what people say. But two weeks ago, a group of around four men set off to deliver a message. They rode out on mules. Four days later, one of the mules came back. So, the Colonel, he gets right mad, starts saying 'those damned Saints, they ain't gonna play me for a tenderfoot', and he goes and orders another six men, one of whom was Sergeant Spencer, a real firecracker of a man, and they go off into the sunset."

"Same message?"

"Yep," said Ableman, "same result too. We ain't ever heard a thing."

"What do you reckon happened to them?"

Winterton shrugged. "They was either killed by the Mormons, or by savages. Either way, they're dead."

"And now you're gonna tell us," said Ableman, his voice a deep, resigned rumble, "that this 'job' you've been offered by the Colonel is to deliver the same goddamned message. Am I right?"

"You are indeed, my friend. You are indeed."

After a night under canvas, listening to the snores of Ableman, with the rocky ground digging into his back, and the heat radiating from the surrounding rocks, Simms managed hardly a wink of sleep and roused himself at dawn, feeling as if a herd of stampeding cattle had pummeled every bone in his body. He washed himself in an area set aside for morning ablutions, then took some breakfast, prepared by the field cook, who studied him, impressed. "My, mister, you're up early."

"Couldn't sleep." He took the proffered plate of thick ham slices and two eggs. "This looks good."

"I hope so. Not many ever tell me if it is. Guess they would if it wasn't!"

They both laughed and Simms turned, almost crashing into Lieutenant Calhoon chomping on a dead cigar. He appeared bedraggled and unshaven, shirt hanging out of his trousers, but his eyes were keen, sharp as flint. "You leave in less than a quarter of an hour, detective."

"Good job I got first in line," Simms said, nodding at his breakfast. "Might be the last decent meal I have for a time."

"You can head out with those two city-dwellers you've fallen in with."

"I'm not so sure that's such a good idea. I prefer working on my own."

"I don't want to take the risk of you deciding to forget the message and continue on your own sweet way. Call it my guarantee."

"Fair enough, but not them two. They're too green. I want two good men. Men who know what they're doing."

Calhoon frowned. "You expecting trouble? Had yourself a premonition?"

"You've already sent two groups out, and neither has come back. They're almost certainly dead, killed by Indians more than likely. Utes are mean, Lieutenant. They don't take prisoners."

"What do you know about Utes?"

"Enough. Came across them during the war, used some as scouts. They led us a merry dance, ran us straight into an ambush. Mexicans weren't the only ones who wanted us dead."

"But you survived."

"I did. Not without some effort. If I'm going up against them again, I want men who can kill without flinching. Men who can fight, men who can survive. When I return, you can give me those two to help me check out that ranch you talked about. That's their limit, I reckon."

"You're all heart, ain't you detective?"

"No. I simply want someone guarding my back, is all."

"Very well, I'll assign you a couple of regulars." He pulled out a timepiece from his waistcoat pocket, flipped open the lid and chewed the cigar. "You got ten minutes from now. Meet me by the command tent with all your belongings." He snapped the lid shut. "And don't be late."

Simms made his farewells to his two bed-fellows and they stood silent and grim, watching him stroll away. They barely said a word to him, except for Ableman who shook his hand. "You take care out there, mister."

Simms appreciated that. "Thanks. Don't you get too bored sitting around here with nothing to do. When I get back, I might even buy you boys a drink."

And now, standing waiting outside Colonel Johnston's command tent, he itched to be off, back on the trail, to get this job done, then find Elisabeth Randall. And the two desperadoes who took her. Retribution was within reach.

Ten

Mason found a cluster of around twenty or so buildings, half a day's journey from the ranch where he'd left Elisabeth. Most appeared empty, or abandoned, but several showed signs of occupancy, with one or two appearing to be newly painted. No one moved in the street, however, and an eerie silence clung to every part of this strange, dormant township. He tied the wagon up outside an imposing cattle association building and strode in, without pausing to brush off the dust clinging to every fiber of his clothing.

The room was big, square and very dark. There were two rows of desks opposite each other, forming a sort of avenue leading to the far end where a much wider desk stood on top of a stage. This allowed anyone who sat there to have a good view of the entire area, especially those others who might work at the accompanying, smaller desks. For the moment, the only workers were a few men at their desks, stooped over gigantic ledgers, scribbling with ink pens.

Mason stood and stared, a little in awe of the size of the room. Against the left wall, a staircase led up to the top story and he made as if to approach it.

"Can I help you?"

Mason gave a small start and looked across to the nearest clerk behind his desk. He wore a black waistcoat, shirt sleeves rolled up past his elbows, spectacles perched on the end of his nose. His expression was that of a man whose patience might snap at any moment. Mason stepped closer, leaning across the table with his palms planted squarely on the top.

"I need a doctor."

"We handle receipts, notices and accounts for the Pilcher Cattle Association. We're not doctors."

"Where can I find one?"

"In a hospital, I shouldn't wonder."

Mason breathed, teeth gritted. "And where might I find one of those?"

The man spread out his hands. He smiled. "Who knows."

Mason's own patience ran out at that point. He struck quick as a rattler, his hand a blur, the pistol materializing in his hand as if he'd performed a magician's trick. He pressed the barrel into the man's forehead, right between his eyes. "I'll ask you again, and this time I want a helpful answer. *Where do I find a doctor*?"

The clerk whimpered, blood draining from his face, all bravado gone in a blink. Mason heard the shuffling of chairs, the raising of alarmed voices behind him. Without moving the barrel, he looked over his shoulder to see several of the clerk's colleagues standing up, their expressions fearful.

"You just stay real still," said Mason, "or your friend here loses his head." To give greater emphasis to his words, he eased back the hammer of his Navy Colt, and turned his gaze back to the clerk, whose whimpering was growing louder by the second. "Now, tell me nice and slowly where I can find a doctor."

* * *

When the door opened, a young woman stood there, aghast, as Mason pushed past her without saying a word. Newhart lay like a child in his arms, head lolling, skin the color of chalk. The wound in his leg was suppurating, trails of dried, black blood and pus mingling with the fibers of his trousers where Elisabeth's bullet had entered. Mason, breathing hard, stopped halfway down the hall and glared at the woman. "They said there is a doctor here."

"Yes, yes there is," she said and squeezed past him, calling, "Ned, Ned! Come quickly!"

And Ned did come quickly. A young man, neatly dressed, well-groomed and clean-shaven, emerged from a rear room. He took one look at Mason and his burden, and ushered him into a very bright room with a ceiling of glass panels, and so clean it seemed to shimmer.

There was couch in the corner and Ned motioned for Mason to lay Newhart upon it. The young man immediately went up to Mason's stricken companion and put his palm flat against his forehead. He then eased away some of the material from the wound. He pulled in a breath. "Dear God. How long has he been like this?"

"Got shot yesterday."

Ned nodded and shot a glance over to the door, where the woman stood. "I need hot water, towels, and my instruments. Tell Mr. Crossland I will get back to him as soon as I can." The woman disappeared and Ned returned to examining the wound. "It's festering. The bullet looks deep. Heavy caliber. Not good, friend." He stood straight and for the first time, studied Mason. "How did this happen?"

"We got caught in a fire-fight," began Mason, his voice confident. He would tell no lies, merely play around with the truth. "Some people tried to kill us. My friend here caught this one in the leg."

"And you?"

"I'm fine."

Ned paused, searching Mason's face. Then he nodded. "Very well. I'll do what I can, but he's lost a lot of blood, and I can't guarantee—"

"Save him, Doc. Don't let him die." Mason drew back his coat tails and Ned let his gaze settle on the gun at his hip. "This is not something to be negotiated over."

Ned, not taking his eyes off the gun, swallowed hard. "Mister, I'm not a doctor. I'm a vet."

"A what?"

"A veterinarian. I deal with sick animals. I'm employed by the Pilcher Cattle Company to look after their herd and the cowboys' horses. I've never extracted a bullet."

"Then you better learn fast." Mason nodded towards Newhart. "If he dies, so will you."

* * *

For the next few hours, Mason sat on a hard-backed chair in the hallway, leaning forward, elbows resting on his knees, staring, waiting. Around him, the woman and Ned flittered in and out of his periphery vision, sometimes saying things, sometimes not. More than once, he heard Newhart cry out and when he screamed, Mason almost got to his feet. But he resisted, remained on his chair, put his head back against the wall and closed his eyes.

He must have drifted off to sleep, for when the hand shook him and he sat up, everything appeared blurry, out of focus. Disorientated, he went to stand and something hard pushed him back down into his seat. He blinked repeatedly, shook his head, and his surroundings slowly grew clearer.

Three men stood before him, big men, large hats, dustcoats that dropped to their boots. Two stood behind the shoulders of the nearest, who had used a muzzle-loading carbine to press Mason up against the wall. His teeth were chipped and black when he opened his mouth to speak.

"You take it easy, friend," said the man with the gun.

"You came into my offices," snapped one of the others, a thin, gangly individual with snow-white hair and the largest broom-handle moustache Mason thought he'd ever seen.

"Your what?"

"You barged into my office and threatened one of my employees. Nobody does that, sir. This is a law-abiding community, and we do not take kindly to your sort."

Mason narrowed his eyes. "My friend was shot up. I had no choice."

"Well, your friend's a lot better now." It was Ned, hovering in the background, the young woman at his side. She was smiling. "I reckon he'll be fit to travel in a couple of days. But the next twenty-four hours are going to be critical if he is—"

"Shut the fuck up, Wallis," snapped the snow-haired man, "we're not interested in the well-being of that sonofabitch," he snapped his head around to glare at Mason, "nor you. I'm not going to tolerate bastards like you riding in here thinking you can do whatever you want."

Mason grinned back at the older man. "Is that right?"

"Yes, it goddamned well is. I'm going to teach you and your friend a lesson you're never going to forget. Now get to your feet, before I smash your skull in where you sit."

"Mr. Pilcher," interjected Ned, somewhat hesitantly, "this gentleman's friend should not be moved. Not for at least—"

"I told you to *shut up*. Get him ready. We're taking them both to the jail and tomorrow, we're going to have us a public flogging."

Mason groaned. He knew too well the stories of these remote settlements, with their almost Biblical sense of justice. He also knew he would never succumb to such indignity. "Ah shit," he growled and attacked. He slapped away the carbine and slammed his boot into the first man's groin. The other two tried to react, but Mason was moving too fast. A big man, he had the grace of a dancer, dipping and swerving, the Navy Colt in his grip, and he shot the second man in the chest, throwing him back against the wall opposite. Pilcher squealed and Mason struck him across the jaw with the revolver, span around, put a bullet through the first man's temple and watched him crumple, brains spewing out across the lovely, bright white paintwork of the hallway.

The woman took to screaming, a single, prolonged wail of horror and Mason glowered in her direction, struck out his right arm ramrod straight, easing back the hammer of the Colt. "You stop that now. I ain't going to harm you, not if I don't have a need to." The woman immediately stopped and fell into Ned's arms, who held her close, his terrified eyes locked on Mason's gun.

Mason turned his attention to Pilcher, who was on his knees, breathing hard, blood dripping from his broken mouth, and levelled the gun against the old man's head. "You're one self-righteous bastard," said Mason. "How many men you got in this town?"

Pilcher muttered something, but his words made little sense through broken teeth and a smashed jaw.

"Most of them are probably out on the range," put in Ned quickly. "He'll have a few over at the livery stable, but no more than three or four."

"Armed?"

"I would think so."

Mason grunted. "I'm going over there, with this sorry bastard. Get myself a horse. I want you to put Newhart into the wagon, make him as comfortable as you can. And I want clean dressings so I can tend to him."

"But you can't. He'll bleed out."

"Then you better sew him up with cat gut, Doc, because I ain't looking for him to die on me. You understand?"

"All right, but listen," said Ned, holding the woman even closer to him. She was sobbing now, but a little calmer than earlier. "You must take it slow; any sudden movements will burst the stitches. You're best heading north-west, make to the river. There's a ferry there, about a day and a half's ride away. There are engineers there, doing a survey. They'll have a surgeon, I shouldn't wonder."

"North-west?" Mason chewed at his lip, "Engineers? You mean Federal people? That don't seem like such a good option, Doc."

"You head west, you'll run straight into Indians. They won't parley with you. All of that has long gone. There's trouble in the west, right across the Territory. You go in there; you won't come out alive."

Mason considered his options and soon realized he didn't have any. "Seems like providence has led me this way, Doc. I thank you for your kindness."

"It's no kindness, mister. I just want you gone, out of our lives. Now."

Mason chuckled and lifted Pilcher up by the collar. "Yeah, well, that is understandable." He tipped the brim of his hat with the barrel of his gun. "Sorry for messing up your nice little home." And he went out, dragging Pilcher with him, the old man a dead weight in his grip, but an easy load nevertheless. The man was nothing but skin and bone.

Eleven

Elisabeth stood at the graveside, head down, lips moving in prayer. Beside her, the two young men, with their wives, and another older man, a farmhand. Their hands were clasped in front, eyes closed, the silence in that desolate place palpable.

They buried the old man, with the maid alongside. A simple wooden cross marked their respective places. Engraved into the wood were the dates of their death. Nothing more. No names, no epitaph. A further mound announced a previous death, two years earlier. Elisabeth assumed it must be the burial place of the young men's mother. She didn't ask, did not think it appropriate, not now with their grief so profound.

They trailed back to the house in silence and when they stepped inside, they all stopped and surveyed the mess. Shattered furniture, upturned tables and chairs, broken crockery, family heirlooms, and bullet holes in the walls, allowing shafts of brilliant sunlight to lance through the dusty air, a latticework of light.

Once Mason escaped with Newhart in the wagon, the young men, biting back their tears, gathered up the bodies of the dead, and set about digging the graves. Now, as Elisabeth looked on, they all set about clearing the debris. Their strength and dignity, in the face of such loss, moved her to tears. It was some moments before she joined them.

Much later, the older farmhand served up a thin gruel of beans and potatoes, tasteless, lukewarm. Nobody raised a voice of objection. No one spoke, the slurping of soup and munching of bread the only sounds. Grief was now part of their family.

In the cool of the late evening, one of the women motioned Elisabeth to join her out on the porch. They sat and looked out across the prairie, a myriad of stars twinkling across the blackness, in the distance a coyote making a plaintive howl. Elisabeth dabbed at her forehead with a kerchief, the heat oppressive, constant. The woman smiled. "My name is Ann." She reached over and took Elisabeth's hand in a smooth, firm grasp and Elisabeth smiled in return. "We are a simple family, with..." Ann stopped, biting her lip and her breathing juddered as she caught a sob in her throat. When she continued, her voice had lost its former confidence, the pain of her loss taking its toll. "I'm sorry, we *were* a simple family, living out here in the wild, tending our cattle. My husband Job and his brother Jacob, together with Sarah, his wife. And father Joseph, of course. A tower of strength he was, a man of virtue and wisdom. He was our guide, our rock. And now, he is gone."

"Those men," said Elisabeth, quickly, trying to prevent the woman from breaking down over the enormity of what had happened, "they took me by the barrel of a gun, left my own father for dead. For all I know, he *is* dead. They took me and they brutalized me, out on the prairie, every night. Mason, the one whom I tried to kill, he was the worst. A devil."

"God will bring down his wrath, sister. Have no fear."

Elizabeth brought up her fists, clenched tight, the knuckles showing white under the skin, her voice trembling as she spoke, "Then why did He not strengthen my hand, my aim? I fired six shots, not one struck home."

"There is always a purpose, sister. Do not fret yourself. Justice will be done."

Elisabeth rested her head against the ranch house wall and closed her eyes briefly. She was no longer certain if justice would ever be done. Mason seemed invincible, protected by forces far stronger than anything Ann proclaimed. Nothing sent by God. Mason's violations, excesses and brutality were not human. A beast, sent from hell to reap carnage and suffering to all who crossed his path. That was how she saw him, and she could think of no reason why her thoughts might be wrong. "Justice will be served when I see him dead, in the ground, his heart torn out."

Ann placed her hand on Elisabeth's knee and squeezed. "We are all suffering right now. It will pass. We shall never forget, but the pain will leave and then we will look upon the world with a clearer vision. You're grieving, sister, as we all are. Give it time."

Elisabeth ground her teeth, accepting the wisdom of this woman's words, but not liking what she heard. Her hatred for Mason was the one thing which forced her to survive, to greet each new day with a renewed desire to kill him. All through his constant pounding, those rough hands pawing at her flesh, his slack lips rolling over her mouth, his flanks heaving and thrusting, the image of his death gave her the strength to suffer him. Even when revulsion turned to acceptance, and she would hold him, touch him, reciprocate, the thought of killing him never left her. Now, with him gone from her life, those thoughts grew stronger still. "My grief will only cease once he is dead."

Another squeeze and Ann sat back to study the stars for herself. "This was a beautiful place once. Only yesterday in fact. Somehow, it seems like a lifetime ago."

"Your family, this house and land, who are you? And how have you managed to survive out here?"

"We arrived some three years ago, together with a hundred other families, making our way across the trail to Utah. We had an idea we could start again, rebuild the life denied us back east. A life free from ignorance and hate. We're Mormons, Elisabeth. When we saw this place, it was as if the Lord Himself, Our Heavenly Father, were pointing His finger, saying to us to stay and settle. So we did. With the help of our friends, we built this house, bought stock from the Pilcher ranch, went into partnership with him. He is a good man, a Christian man. Kind, honest and true. He helped us in so many ways. In return we helped graze his cattle, and protect this outlying part of his land from the excesses of the savages, many of whom we have tamed and brought to the true way of the Lord. We have lived in peace with them ever since."

"And the other grave?" Elisabeth nodded her head towards the area of high ground where they'd laid the old man and the maid.

"Our mother, Mary. The pestilence took her less than a year after we settled. For months, all Joseph would do was sit and stare. No words could console him, despite all our best efforts. Then, one morning, he stood and announced his recovery. He took to repainting the entire house with such vigor, it was as if he were a young man once more. The Lord blesses us in so many ways, Elisabeth." Ann smiled and in the darkness, her teeth glowed white. "We have spoken, my husband Job and I, and we are of the same desire – we wish you to join us, Elisabeth, be part of our family."

For a moment, Elisabeth could not find her breath. She sat, unable to speak, Ann's words bringing shock, surprise, even bewilderment. From being out on the open range, suffering weeks of hardship, brutality and fear, to this. Peace. An opportunity to rediscover something of what she once had. She did not know what to say, or even how to say it.

"Take your time. Think about our offer, Elisabeth. Do not rush to a decision now. But it is clear you have not lived well, that your heart is hard, your soul besmirched by hate, but with us, deliverance will be yours. So sleep, and in the morning when you awake and the sunlight brings with it all the hope and happiness of knowing you are home, give us your answer. It is our sincere wish for you to live with us, to share our love for one another and for Our Heavenly Father."

"I know nothing about you or your faith."

"You do not need to. We accept you for who you are and will never ask anything of you. All we desire is your love and acceptance."

"You have those things already."

She smiled. "We want you to be safe, Elisabeth, to put behind you all the dreadful things you have experienced."

"I want for nothing less."

"Then consider our offer, Elisabeth, and stay. Become one of our family."

"No." She did not react to Ann's sharp intake of breath, but set her eyes across the plain. "I can't do that, Ann. I'm not ready. Not even if I sleep and consider it for a hundred years." She leaned across and squeezed Ann's hand. "But I will work as your maid."

"Elisabeth, we would never ask you to—"

"I know. You do not have to say it. I believe you. But, I cannot change who I am, not until that scoundrel lies dead in the ground. So, towards that end, I'll stay here and help you in as many ways as I can." She gave a short laugh as she remembered their evening meal. "I tasted that man's soup. It was disgusting."

"Ah, Peter? Yes, yes, I have to say…" She took up giggling, rocking forward, hand over her mouth, "Forgive me, but yes!"

"I'm a good cook. Father always used to say I'd missed my vocation, that I should head up a fancy restaurant." Elisabeth smiled, shaking her head, images of her father looming up inside her head. She dabbed at her eye with the kerchief. "That man, the one who made the soup, who is he?"

"Peter is our farmhand. He tends to the cattle; the few sheep we have. He feeds the animals, takes them to the market when Mr. Pilcher calls for them, helps with bringing in supplies, repairs fences, all types of different things. He's a rock and we would sorely miss him if he were not here."

"Is he … Is he not one of you?"

"Of our faith?" Ann shook her head. "No. Neither was Suzanna, our maid. But they are blessed, as you are, Elisabeth. I can see it, otherwise I would not have invited you to stay. The rest of our family feel the same, and Peter too. So think on it, Elisabeth, please. Our wish for you to stay and be part of us is sincere."

Elisabeth smiled and sat back in her chair, gazing into the distance. She had no doubt Ann was truthful, generous and good. Perhaps, living here with these people would allow her time to rediscover herself and, just possibly, give her a base where she could stay and wait for Father to return. "I don't need to think on it, Ann. I've made my decision. If you will have me as your cook and maid, I will accept your generous offer."

Ann gave a tiny scream of joy and threw her arms around Elisabeth. She held her with such love, such passion, that Elisabeth broke down and cried.

Twelve

Two men stood at the far end of the street. Both held shotguns. They were silent, feet planted firmly apart, eyes staring ahead. To their right, kneeling in a shop doorway was another man with a handgun, and over to the left, on the roof of a merchant's store, a fourth man trained a muzzle-loading rifle on Mason, who was moving down the street as if out for a Sunday afternoon stroll. None of the men made to fire their weapons. How could they, for to attempt such a thing would be foolish indeed. Mason had Pilcher by the neck, using him as a shield. And Mason was grinning.

He stopped about ten paces or so from the two blocking the street, pulled in a breath, and prodded Pilcher in the temple with the barrel of his own revolver. "Tell you what, boys, you step aside, let me help myself to a horse, and we end all of this without any further nonsense." He eased back the hammer of his gun. Pilcher emitted a tiny cry, a frightened bird, trapped, frantic. "What do you say?"

"I'd say you're a dead man, mister."

Mason whistled, tilting his head to survey the owner of the voice. A tall man, a few days' growth of beard around his chin, wiry, keen-eyed. "Well, if you're willing to see your good boss here die first, then that's just fine and dandy. Your call."

The man beside the first spat onto the ground. "Kill the bastard, Hodge."

Hodge nodded, but made no move with his shotgun, which remained cradled in his hands across his midriff. "Mister, what is it you want?"

"I told you," said Mason, eyes darting to the shop doorway, then to the roof opposite. He estimated once the shooting started, he'd have around five seconds before he received a bullet. Of course, it might be in his arm just as easily as it might be his head, but a bullet would hold him up, make him a perfect target for the others, especially the one called Hodge, who seemed to have something about him. Unless, of course, Mason's good luck held. In which case, it might be worth the risk. "I want a horse. You allow me that, and time to leave this place, and your employer here, he lives."

"Tell us what the shooting was."

"Where's Holness and Rankin?"

Mason shrugged, "If they was the two men with this dear old gentlemen, sorry to say, they are departed."

The man called Hodge blinked, reeled back as if struck, and snapped his head around to his partner. "He killed them."

A tiny tremble flickered in Hodge's eyes. Mason saw it, recognized it for what it was. Mason sighed. "Oh dear."

He put a bullet through Pilcher's brain and was already moving before any of the others reacted. He ran straight for the shop doorway, keeping low, firing from the hip. The man next to Hodge flipped backwards, chest spouting blood. Hodge was screaming, bringing the shotgun to bear. But he was too late. Mason could move faster than any of them expected, and he made the boardwalk before Hodge managed to loose off both barrels, the buckshot spreading wide, but not wide enough to hit Mason.

The man in the doorway stood up and ran, throwing down his weapon. Mason, teeth clamped white in his face, swept up the man's fallen revolver and used it, putting two bullets into the fleeing man's back.

With his own revolver empty, Mason swung around and a musket ball slapped into the doorframe beside him. He glanced across and clicked his tongue, took a bead on the man on the roof and fired, missing him. With two bullets left, he marched into the street, eyes set straight ahead on Hodge fumbling with the shotgun, desperate to feed in new cartridges. His hands shook, his body trembled, and when he raised his head, his eyes were blinking rapidly, stung by thc sweat rolling down his face. "Oh sweet Jesus," he said as a parting speech. He snapped the shotgun closed but it was the last thing he ever did.

Mason shot him at point-blank range through the head and got down beside the body. He searched through the dead man's clothing, found his revolver on his hip and pulled it free from the holster. The gun was a monstrous Walker-Colt, far too heavy for a sidearm, but Mason had little time to admire it, as when he glanced up, another musket ball hit the dirt next to his knee. Closer this time. He trained Hodge's revolver on the shape on the roof, took careful aim, and with plenty of time as the man was reloading, loosed off six, measured shots.

The silence which ensued, was deafening. Mason's ears rang from the explosion of sound from the handgun. He dropped the revolver and jiggled an index finger into his ear. He screwed up his eyes and as the cordite wafted away, he saw two feet sticking out over the edge of the store roof. Wounded or dead, Mason didn't much care what fate had befallen the man. For now, Mason had bought himself valuable time and he made good use of it.

He strode down the deserted street. He thought he caught some movement behind the occasional pane of glass in the stores and other buildings, but he no longer cared. These people, whoever they were, were not about to risk their lives after what they'd witnessed. Not against someone like Mason. Someone so blessed.

* * *

Ned waited in his house doorway, as he had since Mason left, arms folded, lips pressed together, eyes never leaving the street. But his shoulders slumped when he saw the familiar shape of the killer emerging from out of the distance. He'd hoped Mason would die at the hands of Pilcher's men, good men, hardy, experienced. But now, with the devil himself riding tall and straight in the saddle, all those hopes dwindled.

"How is he, Cathy?" he called down the hallway. After a few seconds, Cathy appeared, brushing back a lock of hair from her face, looking drained, tired.

"He's sleeping. Breathing is even, the fever gone. The wound seems clean, but the swelling tells me he'll not walk again without a limp."

Ned nodded and she came up next to him. He slipped his arm around her waist and they both peered towards Mason, approaching with a steady, unhurried tread. "You think we could kill this bastard?"

She gaped up at him, "Don't be a fool, Ned. The man is not human. Look at him, as bold as you like. There isn't a scratch on him. If you go up against him, he'll win, and I don't want you dead. Not like the others. I've never seen anything as terrible as what he did."

"I wonder where Pilcher is?"

"Dead, more than likely. As they all are. The man is some sort of monster, Ned. Let's just do what he says and watch him ride out."

"But what if he won't? What if he means to kill us too?"

"I don't think he will. We helped his friend. He has no cause."

"A man such as he requires no cause, Cathy. He does as he wishes. If he has a mind to kill us, he will."

"Then let us pray he does not have the mind, Ned."

* * *

They did pray, both of them, offering up a silent plea to the heavens to allow them to live. And when Mason got down from his horse and stomped past them without a word, they felt God had answered their prayers. They stood, in silence, and watched Mason return down the hallway, carrying Newhart with nonchalant ease. He went outside and placed his friend in the back of the wagon. He then tied his newly acquired horse to the tail gate, jumped up on the buckboard and twitched the moth-eaten nag ahead of him with the reins. He steered the wagon around to the left, then stopped. He twisted in his seat and put a finger to the brim of his hat. "Thank you for your kindness. There will be men who will come and they will ask you which way I went. You tell them, they will die. Remember that." Then he flicked the reins again and the wagon trundled out across the street in the direction Ned told him to go. Towards the ferry on the river.

Cathy blew out a long breath. "Will you tell them, when they come?"

Ned shook his head. "I would be signing away their lives if I did."

For a long time, they both stood in silence, watching Mason until he was nothing more than a black dot on the horizon.

A noise caused them both to look up. An old man, hat held aloft, came stumbling towards them, bleating like a goat, "Doc, Doc! You have to come, come quick."

Cathy squeezed Ned's arm and went down the steps towards the old man as he drew closer, his face white as chalk, gulping in air, body close to collapse.

"Oh Jonas, dear God Almighty, what is it?"

"It's Mr. Pilcher. Shot. Shot dead, Catherine." He fell into her arms and she helped him to the steps as Ned appeared from inside with a glass of water. The old man took it in fingers as thin and gnarled as willow tree twigs, and he swallowed it down, gasping. "I ain't ever seen anything like it. Not if I live to be a hundred. They fired their guns and not one bullet hit him. But whenever he fired back, they died. And they're all dead, save for Prentice who lies on the roof with his legs bleeding like a fountain." He gripped Cathy's arm, "You have to come, you have to save him."

"They're all dead?" asked Ned.

"All the others, yes. They didn't stand a chance." He put down the glass and covered his face with his hands. "I never want to see anything like it again. Mr. Pilcher. Sweet Jesus, what are we going to do?"

Ned chewed his lip and held Cathy's questioning look. "We can pray," he said at last, turned his face towards the horizon in the direction he knew would lead Mason to the river and wishing he could be there, to watch that devil die.

Thirteen

With the horses and two pack-mules readied, saddlebags and canteen full, Simms took a final meal of eggs and potatoes from the cook, who wished him well, but with the detachment of someone who knows no further meeting would ever take place. Simms then strolled to the tent where he'd slept for the previous two nights, and bade farewell to the men with whom he'd shared his canvas home. Both looked grim, said little, but Simms promised them he would see them again. Neither responded and Simms only smiled.

He left the camp at a slow walk, three soldiers trailing behind him, their blue shirts already soaked with perspiration. None spoke. They set their faces northwest, their mood heavy, resigned.

They continued in silence to higher ground, leaving the dull, flat plain sucked dry by the searing heat far behind, and wound their way up into the hills. They followed a trail already old from the many prospectors and settlers who made their way west, lured by the promise of gold and land. Lately, settlers seeking new opportunities, or religious groups fleeing persecution went this way, using the same, well-trodden highway. Desperadoes, bandits and Indians used it also, but for very different reasons. Simms knew this and kept his senses alert as he and the others settled into a steady pace. Soon, thoughts of camp, prepared food, companionship and safety, dwindled.

Simms led the way, steering his horse along a narrow pathway flanked by jagged rocks, white hot, but affording some welcome shade.

He knew however, by nightfall these same rocks would radiate heat, making sleep virtually impossible. His plan was to keep moving, make the plain again by sundown, find some relief, the faintest hint of cool air.

The first day clawed by, the horses plodding through the thick, dusty earth, their heads bowed. Behind him, the soldiers – silent and sullen – draped themselves over the necks of their mounts. There was no respite from the relentless, slow, merciless ride and boredom, as much as the heat, drove them ever deeper into a mire of depression.

On the morning of the second day, Simms climbed to a vantage point and saw the plain stretching out before him. One of the soldiers had brought with him a telescope, which Simms now used to pick out areas of scrub, a few withered trees. On the far, distant horizon, a tiny trail of smoke caught his attention. He lowered the glass, twisting his mouth into a snarl. Perhaps the smoke came from a campfire, tenderfoots journeying deeper into the Territory, seeking out a promised land, with no laws to govern or restrict. And no protection either.

He snapped the eyeglass together. The likelihood was, he mused grimly, the fire came from Indians. Utes. A camp, or more disturbingly, a homestead, attacked and destroyed. He sighed, pulled off his hat and wiped his brow with the back of his hand.

The men were breaking camp, packing away equipment, food, checking weapons. They all glanced up as Simms came down from the hillside.

"We will reach the plain in less than an hour." He studied each solider in turn. "If you thought it was hot yesterday, what we're about to reach will test all our endurance. Keep your heads down and try your best to conserve water."

"How long will it take us to cross?"

Simms shrugged, looking again to the west. From here, the smoke was invisible. "A day."

"This is horse shit," said one of them.

Simms arched an eyebrow. "What's your name, soldier."

"Hanson. Corporal Hanson.

"Well, Corporal, we're all in this shit together. We have no choice. We just have to accept it for what it is."

Hanson grumbled, looked askance at the others. "And when we get there?"

"*If* we get there," said another. He noted Simms's questioning stare. "Wicks. My name is Private Wicks. This here is Landers." The third soldier stiffened slightly but remained quiet. "We were ordered to accompany you, mister, but none of us are happy about it."

"We all know about the other groups who were sent," added Hanson. "This smacks of a suicide mission."

"Well, it ain't," said Simms. He put his hands on his hips and moved his head to the west. "Something happened out there, to both sets of men. They either got lost and died of thirst, or," he looked to the soldiers again, "somcone killed them."

"Mormons?"

Simms shrugged. "Could be. Or Utes. We'll know soon enough, I reckon. So, if you hear me holler, you move to cover, you understand?" They all nodded, not one looking away. "Because if it's Utes we come up against, you need to know those bastards are meaner than the sun overhead, boys. And control your fire, make every shot count. We have no idea how many there are out there, but this is their land, no matter what Brigham Young might say. They were here long before any of us even dreamed about this place, before any white man, be he devil or a son of God, came to this land. It's theirs and they want to keep it that way. So, sleep if you can, but keep an ear open for my shout."

He slunk over to his horse and swung the saddle across its back. Already the heat pulsed through the air.

They camped later amongst bracken and scree, throwing themselves down in the dirt without blankets, exhausted, drained from the journey across the unrelenting plain. Simms sipped from his canteen and put his head back against his saddle, the only one amongst the party who prepared some kind of makeshift bed. His blanket lay close, for he knew in a few hours the temperature would drop as the rocks were no longer nearby. He took time to hobble the horses, keeping them close. He knew well enough how the Natives could traverse the ground in total silence, bellies close to the earth, slithering like snakes. They would come and take the horses within a blink of an eye and none of the soldiers would know of it until the morning came. So Simms kept the animals within an arm's reach, and his Colt Dragoon in his hand, slept fitfully, stirring every few moments to check the darkness.

As the sun rose above the horizon and any more chance of rest withered in the blazing heat, the men rose themselves, prepared breakfast, sat and munched. Simms again stepped out into the open and fixed the telescope to the west. No evidence of the smoke remained and he scanned the endless vista for any other signs. There was nothing and he allowed his breath to trickle out, the tension leaving his shoulders. For now.

They cut out across the plain, the features of the landscape slowly changing, from hard, coarse, broken rock and scree to more giving, albeit parched, grassland. It rose gently, rolling hillsides pressing in around them, and the air slowly grew fresher. "It's the river," breathed Simms, twisting in his saddle to smile at the others. "Half a day maybe. The worst is behind us."

Or so he believed.

After a brief rest in an area dotted with blackened, withered trees, they cut through a dip in the hills and came upon a glade, where the soil had been tilled, perhaps only weeks before. And across from these fields, prepared by the sweat and toil of settlers, stood a cabin. But not a tranquil, homely place. A place of death.

The timbers were charred, the roof collapsed, main door kicked in. The entire building was gutted, the thick, acrid smell of burning wood filling everyone's nostrils as they drew closer.

Simms reined in his horse and his eyes roamed across the surrounding hills. Without a word, he pulled out the carbine from its sheath and slipped from the saddle. "Fan out, Wicks to the left, Henson to the right. Go wide, and keep your eyes peeled. Landers, you come with me."

The soldiers, used to obeying orders, quickly spread out, and Simms ran, bent double, to a fenced-in vegetable patch, where he stopped, kneeling and watching. Landers beside him, breathing hard, whispered, "Who did this?"

"Utes," said Simms.

"How do you know? Maybe it was them Mormons?"

Simms shook his head, motioning towards the cabin walls. When Landers followed his gaze he saw them for himself; several arrows protruding from the woodwork, blackened twigs, but still recognizable. Landers grunted and Simms gave him a quick glance. "Stay alert. I'm going inside, you cover me. Understand?"

Landers nodded and Simms saw how the young soldier's lips trembled. He squeezed his forearm, winked, then moved forward in a zigzag pattern, keeping low, carbine ready.

Reaching the doorway, he pressed himself against what was left of the wall. This close, the smell was sharp and thick, smarting his eyes, so he deftly pulled up his neckerchief to cover mouth and nose, took a breath, and chanced a glance inside.

He saw them. Two bodies, adults, twisted into grotesque attitudes, their charred bodies like clumps of brittle charcoal, mouths open in silent screams. If they were once human, this was the only sign they bore of who they might have been, their features fused into a single piece of roasted flesh. He swung away and vomited into the dirt, gasping for breath.

Landers ran up next to him, dropping to his knees, eyes scanning the hillside for a moment before nodding to the doorway. "Holy shit, what the hell is in there?"

Simms shook his head, ripping away his neckerchief to wipe his mouth. He slid down the wall, pressing his head back against the black timbers. "Don't go in."

Landers stared, eyes wide, moisture filling up along the bottom lids. "What the fuck?"

The lawman took a breath and stuffed his neckerchief into his pocket. He licked his lips, throat raw from the bile still clinging there, burning him. He swallowed. "I need a drink." He scoured the fields, eyes narrowing. "They might still be here. I thought I saw smoke yesterday. This must have been why."

"You saw it? How?"

"Through the 'scope. I didn't think..." He caught the fury in Lander's face. "I wasn't to know. And besides, what could we have done?"

"Prepared ourselves." Landers closed his eyes. "Jesus. How many are there in there?"

"Two. Adults, possibly. It's hard to tell."

"Likely to be others. Children maybe?"

"I hope to God, no. If there were, the Utes would have taken them. Teenagers too, girls especially. Slaves. It's common practice."

"*Slaves*? Dear God... I didn't know they did such things."

Simms grunted and went to speak, but before he could form the words, Hanson's voice screamed out, "*Simms! Get your ass around here.*"

He exchanged a look with Landers, then the pair of them were skirting around the remains of the cabin towards the sound of the corporal's voice.

Hanson stood a little way off, open to the elements, his carbine held loose by his side, his other hand gripping his hat. He did not move as Simms and Landers came up alongside.

Simms saw it. A young man, no more than twenty, stripped naked, his body propped up against a rock. There was an arrow where his genitals used to be, a burned arrow. They'd split his stomach, grotesque ropes of black, roasted flesh spreading out in a crude arc over the wreck of his abdomen. His eyes, like prunes, plucked out, crusted blood rolling, like slug trails, down his face.

"Why the hell did they do this?"

Landers fell to his knees and quietly sobbed.

Simms drew in a shuddering breath. "Revenge. Punishment. Who knows. There is usually a reason. One thing is for sure, the Mormons had no hand in this."

"You can't know that for sure," snarled Hanson, his eyes wet when he turned his face to consider Simms. "I've heard it say they made peace with these bastards, converted them, gave them the promise of eternal life if they did their dirty work for them."

"There's no reason why any white folk would consent to this, whoever they are or whatever they believe."

"No, not white folk, their servants. The white folk just closed their eyes and minds to it." Hanson turned and spat onto the ground, put his hat back on his head and gritted his teeth. "Every one of these bastards I find, I'm gonna kill. I couldn't give a good damn who they are. They're dead."

He whirled away and strode back across the fields towards where the horses stood.

Simms watched him go and blew out a long breath.

They buried the three bodies as best they could in shallow graves, working through the already prepared earth at the front of the homestead with their knives. Once they covered the bodies with a thin scattering of soil, they placed stones and larger rocks to create mounds and rammed in crudely-fashioned crosses to mark where the dead lay. Wicks said a prayer and they stood in grim silence, considering what had passed.

No words were uttered as they moved away, none of them looking back, all deep within their own thoughts. For a brief period, a clump of clouds drifted across the sky to dim the sun, but only briefly. It was enough to dampen their mood still further.

They crossed the prairie slowly, a ragged procession, heads down, heat draining all the energy from men and beasts alike. They climbed another rock-strewn hill and when they reached the top, they saw below them, in the flat plain, the remains of a camp. They reined in their horses and stood in a line across the rise. Simms leaned forward, put the telescope to his eye and picked out the details. He sucked in his breath. "Shit."

"What the hell is it now?" asked Landers.

"More deaths?" Hanson questioned.

Simms looked across at Hanson and pulled a face. "It's the remnants of a camp. There's a horse, dead. Other bodies alongside."

"Oh Christ," said Wicks and put a hand over his face.

"They're soldiers," said Simms.

The silence spread over them, accompanied by cold air, like ice, causing them all to shiver. Simms gnawed at his lips and nodded to Landers. "You stay with the horses. Do *not* leave them for any reason. You hear or see anything, you yell. Yell like a fucking banshee, you understand?" Landers nodded and Simms got down from his horse, checking his carbine. He narrowed his eyes. "We walk down real slow. Check for any cover and, once you find some, you keep its position in your head. If any shooting starts, you get to that cover and you kill whatever you see."

The other two grunted and dropped down beside him. Together they shuffled down the gentle incline towards the dead.

There were four of them in all, contorted in the hideous aspects of violent death, stomachs bloated, flesh green-black, burned in the sun. Their eyes stared sightlessly towards the sky, one of them squashed up behind the dead horse. There were no weapons, no supplies, and arrows perforated each corpse.

"They took their guns," said Simms, squatting down to run his fingers through the remains of the fire. "Cold," he said and looked to his left, then right. "This might be a war-party, or a hunting-party. Either way, they must have come upon these men hard and fast."

"Ambushed them like the cowardly dogs they are," said Hanson.

"What do you expect, a stand up fight, facing each other in nice, tidy ranks, like the Redcoats of old?"

"You reckon these were the boys General Randall sent out to give his message to the ferry?"

"This is one of the groups, I reckon." Simms stood. He rolled his shoulders. "Strange there ain't no buzzards."

"Eh?" Hanson responded with a frown.

"These bodies, why ain't they been picked clean by the birds?"

Hanson frowned and studied one of the corpses. Something had been pulling away at the soft flesh of the dead man's throat and cheeks. "Well, they did get started."

"Yeah, but not anymore." Simms swiveled on his haunches. "We best pull back, get to the higher ground and—"

Abruptly, Wicks threw up his arms and screamed, falling to his knees. Simms reacted first, rolling across the earth, making himself flat, and levelled his carbine toward the hillside as Wick fell beside him, face down in the dirt, an arrow protruding from his back. He was moaning, tried to push himself upright, and then a second arrow slapped into the back of his skull and he collapsed with a loud sigh, dead.

Hanson was running, revolver in his hand, firing off bullets in the precise opposite reaction to the instructions given to him by Simms. For himself, Simms cursed, and pressed himself up against his dead companion, placing the carbine over Wicks' shoulder, scouring the surroundings for any movement.

And movement followed swiftly.

He saw Landers on the hillside less than one hundred paces away, watched him stand up, carbine held out between two hands, blocking a downward strike by a wild, naked Ute armed with hatchet and knife. Landers twisted, kicked the native in the groin and swung the carbine across his head. Simms saw the Ute drop, but before Landers could do any more, another jumped on his back, bronzed thighs wrapping around him, one arm jerking back his head, the other arm brandishing a hatchet. It would soon be over.

Simms shot the Ute in the head, saw the plume of pink blood, watched him crumple, still wrapped around a frantic, hysterical Landers. Simms feverishly loaded up the Halls with another round, working the paper cartridge into the breech and pressing it shut, ignoring the sweat dripping into his eyes.

He looked up. Landers was bent double on his knees, blowing out his cheeks, winded, terrified. A third Ute reared up and kicked him full in the face, throwing him into the air. The soldier hit the edge of the hillside and pitched over, rolling down in a wild jumble of arms and legs. The Ute sprang after him, knife ready and Simms blew a hole in his throat and sent him into oblivion.

He stood up, discarding the carbine, and pulled out his Colt Dragoon. Nothing else moved, the echo of the gunfire dissipating in the vastness of that place, the only sound the low, pain-filled bleating of Landers, lying on his back, nose and mouth smashed and bleeding.

"Are there more?"

It was Hanson, crammed in behind an outcrop of rock, reloading his revolver as best he could, hands trembling with no seeming strength in any of the fingers, breathing hard through his open mouth.

"Maybe."

Simms took a step forward and relieved Hanson of the revolver. As his, eyes scanned the crest of the hill, he methodically poured powder into each chamber, fitted the shot and pressed home the percussion caps. "They will have taken the horses if there were more of them. The food and water, too." He groaned, gave back the revolver and shuffled over to Landers. He got down next to him. The man's eyes were rolling, the blood leaking from his broken face. Simms took a breath."Did they take the horses?"

Landers blinked a few times, shaking his head once. "Water."

Simms sighed and shouted across to Hanson, "Get him water," before he straightened and made his way slowly up to the crest.

The Ute Landers kicked was lying there in a tight ball, hands clamped at his groin, face swollen where the carbine had smashed into him. The horses had run off, but stood a mere twenty or thirty paces away, quiet, feeding on tufts of coarse grass. They pricked their ears and lifted their heads as Simms slowly approached, soothing them with cooing sounds, stroking their necks, calming them.

He looked back at the hill and saw Hanson, who stood, feet planted wide, one of the hatchets in his hand. Simms watched as Hanson, slowly at first, but increasingly more uncontrolled, hacked the stricken native to pieces, his hand a blur.

Fourteen

Three of them now stood at the graveside, Landers, unable to keep his grief at bay, cried openly whilst Hanson clutched his hat in front of him in both hands, screwing up the rim, teeth clenched. The dead Utes they burned.

"The smoke will warn any others," muttered Hanson, "and I hope more of them come. I truly do."

Simms ignored him and tended to the horses. A little way off, hobbled behind another outcrop of rocks, he came upon some ponies, pulled off their blankets and let them run free across the plain. Three ponies for the three dead Utes. He stared after them for a long time.

The only cross which bore any kind of inscription was the one marking their dead companion's grave. It said simply 'Wicks, a soldier'. Simms thought it was enough.

They rode on in silence, each burdened by their thoughts and the horrors they had witnessed. Simms, who had experienced so many deprivations during the Mexican War, accepted the deaths as a normal part of hostilities. He neither mourned nor harbored thoughts of revenge. His duty was to find Elisabeth Randall and ultimately, nothing would sway him from that path. Once he'd discharged his orders to contact Ives at the Colorado River ferry, he would again head back to the ranch where he felt sure he would find the kidnapped daughter of Colonel Randall. On the way, if he picked up the trail of Newhart and Mason, so much better. Their bounty would ease the remaining journey.

The landscape continued to change, the air thinner and fresher, green grass replacing coarse scrub and when, at last, they left the rolling hills behind, they gazed in abject relief at the great silver snake of the river, wending its way through the land. And at the jetty, moored alongside a rickety gangplank, the riverboat bobbed in the water, as if it were waiting patiently for their arrival.

Simms spurred his horse and, together with the others swiftly following, they ate up the remaining distance, eager to meet with the surveyor there, Lieutenant Joseph Christmas Ives.

As they drew closer, Simms became aware of the shirt-sleeved men around the boat, shouldering rifles, taking aim, and of the man sporting a huge broad-brimmed straw hat of brilliant white, standing in the lead, a revolver in each hand.

Simms with his hand up, ordered the others to slow to a trot, and he called out, "We are Federal officers, sent by Colonel Johnston to deliver a message to your commanding officer."

His voice rang out across the open space between the two groups and for a moment, it seemed as if the entire world held its breath, waiting for Ives's response.

The man in the hat stepped forward, the revolvers held loosely in his hands. "I'm Ives," he said, his voice clear and strong. He nodded towards Simms's companions. "You look like government troops, but I can't be sure. Slip off your firearms and get down from your horses." He lifted his own guns slightly, easing back the hammers, "Nice and easy, boys."

Hanson and Landers shot Simms a glance and the Pinkerton nodded. "Do as he says."

So they did. As Simms relieved himself of his own weapons, some of the men standing close to Ives whistled.

Simms jumped to the ground.

"That's quite an arsenal you have there," said Ives, stepping closer. "What are you, a bounty hunter?"

Simms let his breath out in a long, tired stream. "Pinkerton."

"Good God," said Ives, mouth dropping open. He looked back to his own men. "Boys, lower your guns. No one would say they were a Pinkerton if they were not." He smiled at Simms. "Let's see your license."

Simms brought out the wallet, with his badge pinned inside. Ives leaned forward to study the wording. "That's impressive," he said, and at last, holstered his revolvers. "Can't be too careful, Detective. Boys," he looked across at Hanson and Landers, "collect up your things and one of my men will give you some food and water." He sniffed. "And a bath too. How long you been on the range?"

"Three days," said Simms, "but it feels longer."

"You can tell me about it," said Ives, and led Simms to the boat and his office.

Fifteen

Mason stopped the wagon and chewed the inside of his cheek. He looked back the way he had come. Once news of Pilcher's killing reached the vet's ears, promises and agreements would fly away like paper in the wind. He'd tell, tell them all and Mason didn't want no posse on his trail, no lynch-mob eager to stretch his neck. Newhart's neither. He'd made a mistake, should have put kindness and gratitude aside and shot him. The sister, too. Pity, because she was pretty. *What the hell, there are plenty more lovely things out on the range!* He spat and turned the wagon about.

He couldn't rush, the nag simply did not have the strength to move quicker than a shuffle, but when he arrived back at the surgery, he was relieved to find the surrounding streets empty. The door was open, as it always seemed to be. Mason jumped down and went through into the hallway. He heard a low, pleasant sound of someone singing towards the back of the house. The girl. He smiled and sauntered down the hall.

When she turned from the kitchen sink to see him standing there, her own smile froze on her lips.

Mason's eyes narrowed. "Where's your brother?"

"He's in the surgery. Tending to the one man you didn't kill."

Mason nodded, twisting his mouth into something like a smile. "You are a mighty fine woman, has anyone ever told you that?"

"If you're going to do it, mister, do it. Don't talk."

He nodded in agreement, pulled out his gun, and shot her through the head.

Mason studied her for a moment, a pang of regret playing around his conscience. But he put it aside and was about to stride back down to the other rooms when Ned came blustering out of his surgery door. He gawped in abject horror when he saw Mason and the gun. His shoulders sagged, face going white.

"I can't risk you saying something," said Mason.

Ned nodded, a single tear rolling down his face. "I tried so hard to make a life here, for my sister and me. I thought we'd made something, something to be proud of. For it to end like this…" He put his fingers in his eyes and sobbed.

"I know," said Mason and fired his gun, two times.

He stepped over the body, careful not to put his boot into the blood blooming over the floor, and went into the surgery.

The man on the bed strained his neck to stare Mason in the eye. "Bastard," he managed, before Mason shot him too.

Back at the wagon, Mason sat for a moment, playing with the reins. The death of the sister troubled him. Handsome, tall, face of an angel. She reminded him a little of Elisabeth and the thought of her, the moments they'd spent together, caused his chest to tighten. "Damn it," he said out loud, flicked the nag into continuing forward, memories stirring of how she'd writhe beneath him. How could she change into the murderous harlot she was, trying to shoot him back at the Mormon ranch? Could it be she was play-acting through it all? He ground his teeth, struggling to beat down the rising anger. He couldn't afford to go back there to the ranch, not now. Too many people wanted him dead, too many were no doubt already on his trail. No, he'd have to keep going forward, get to the ferry, and try to acquire some money. He needed a new life, a new start. A few more killings, then all would be as he'd always wanted it.

By the time they made camp that first night, any memories of Elisabeth and regrets for Cathy's death were long gone.

* * *

Four riders stood motionless on the distant ridge the following afternoon, like black statues set against a backdrop of unsullied sky. A disturbing image, designed to frighten, intimidate. Mason pulled on the reins and the weary nag shuffled to a halt. He considered the men for a long time. Keeping his eyes locked on the strangers, Mason slowly uncorked his canteen and drank. From this distance, it was impossible to make out who the riders might be, but he guessed they were Utes. He had a vague idea of where he was, but knew if he had wandered too far west, trouble was bound to be waiting. He was also well aware of the many stories of attacks, raids, killing. Why the Mormons back at the ranch fared so well in such a hostile land, he could not imagine. Perhaps they truly were blessed? He pushed the stopper back into the canteen and tossed it into the wagon. Newhart moaned.

He swung down from the buckboard and stretched his limbs. With a quick glance towards the horizon where the sun slowly sank, he decided to make camp for the night. If the Utes came close, he'd kill them. Better to be safe than sorry. Experience had taught him not to take chances with Indians.

He went around to the rear of the wagon, patted the tethered horse, checking its flanks and its hooves. The mare snuffled but otherwise appeared fit and well. Then he took a peep inside.

Newhart lay outstretched on his back, his filthy shirt soaked with sweat, his head lolling from side to side. Blood and pus seeped from his leg. Mason swore, stepped away from the rear opening and spat onto the ground. The coming night would prove to be long, Newhart's fever about to hit a crescendo. He looked to the far-off ridge and a slight flutter ran through his heart.

The Utes had gone.

* * *

Supper was a meagre affair of oatmeal biscuits and salted beef strips, which he gnawed at until his jaw ached and washed it all down with water. He shook the canteen. Not much left. If he didn't make the river in two more days, he could die from thirst out here. He sat with his back against the rear wheel of the wagon, revolver in his lap, and wished he had a smoke. He wished for lots of things. Mostly, he wished to be at the river and safety. He was growing tired of forever having to watch his back.

Deciding against lighting a fire, he gathered a threadbare blanket around his shoulders and tried to make himself comfortable. Behind him, on the other side of the canvas, Newhart's moans grew louder. Mason did his best to block them out, pulled his hat down hard over his face and closed his eyes.

If he slept, it could not have been for long. He awoke with a start, body tense, hand automatically bringing up his Navy Colt. Night had settled over the camp, the sky a glittering sprinkle of stars, the air colder than at any other time. He eased back the hammer as slow as he could manage. He listened and waited. For a moment, his own heartbeat was the only sound, then the tiniest of footfalls stirred him and he sat rigid and silent as stone, readying himself.

Perhaps a breath, a wheeze, a snuffle. Whatever the sound, it betrayed the close proximity of another human being. And not Newhart. His moans were less now, the rattle in his chest different to this other noise.

The horse whinnied and shuffled its hooves. Over by some withered trees, the nag, hobbled, resting, also gave out a strange, strangulated neigh. Both animals reacting to something – or someone – very close.

He caught sight of a shadow from the corner of his eye, nothing more than a flicker of grey in the blackness of the night. He remained rigid, mouth open, senses alert.

It came from out of the night at a run, a rushing thing, no scream, only the pounding of its feet on the stony ground. A man. Mason half-rose and caught him around the throat, wrestled him to the ground, the barrel of his gun jabbing into the flesh of his assailant's hard stomach.

He writhed and kicked, a hand raised, filled with the glint of a blade. Mason pulled his hand from the throat, caught the wrist, squeezed the trigger and the night's silence splintered with the blast.

And the others.

They attacked from three sides, wild demons erupting out of the blackness. Mason, on his feet, fanned his gun's hammer and shot the first one charging forward with a spear held in both hands. He crumpled to the ground, body riddled with the bullets, his forward momentum propelling him across the dirt to stop inches from Mason's feet.

Mason whirled and clubbed the second with the revolver, all bullets spent. The native pitched forward, dropping to his knees and Mason hit him a second time across the top of the skull. But the third gave him no time to prepare. Mason fell with the weight of his assailant, his lithe body, slick with sweat, wrapping around him. Desperate, Mason lashed out with fists, saw the flash of steel, managed to grab the descending arm and wrestled him to the side. He swung up his knee, felt the man's body go limp, a tiny moan gurgling from deep inside and Mason ripped the knife from his grip and plunged it into his attacker's throat, not once, but three, four times. The blood flooded over his hand, thick, hot, gushing like a fountain. He threw the knife away, disgusted.

It was over.

Mason stood, breathing hard, half expecting another Ute to attack. But there was nothing, only the horrible chasm of the night's blackness swallowing everything up. Not far off, the horses were wild, kicking, screaming, and the entire wagon rocked from side to side. Newhart roused, calling out, "Oh Christ, Mama, they're here. They're here, Mama!"

Mason lowered his breathing. The second fallen Indian at his feet was groaning. Mason's blow to the top of the Ute's head may well have shattered the skull. Perhaps he would die, perhaps not. Feverishly, Mason reloaded his gun, but his actions were careless, precious powder spilling onto the ground. He cursed, eyes flickering this way and that, sure there were more of them. Finally, with the last cap fitted onto the nipple, he twirled the cylinder, coked the hammer and peered out into the darkness.

Then he heard it. The hasty retreat of a horse's hooves, pounding across the prairie, disappearing into the night.

He allowed himself a long sigh, ran a hand across his brow. The surviving Indian groaned again and Mason, holstering his revolver, went to the fallen spear of the first dead Indian, returned and sank its point deep into the wounded Ute's neck. Mason felt the man wriggle and writhe, heard the sound of bubbling blood, and pressed ever deeper until the body went slack. Leaving the spear sticking out from the body, he staggered over to the horse, and ran gentle caresses across its neck. When at last it grew quieter, he drank from his canteen, draining it, no longer caring it was the last of the water. He held onto the tailgate, put his head down, and waited for the trembling to stop.

* * *

The next day, Newhart sat up, the fever broken, his eyes alert, curious. Mason sat down beside him in the back of the wagon and grinned. "Good to have you back, old friend."

"I heard things," said Newhart, "or dreamed them, I know not which. I saw my dear old mother shaking and a-screaming, telling me the Lord's justice would come." He ran both hands through his lank hair. "It was awful, Mason. I've never had such dreams before. And shooting, there was shooting."

"That was me. We were attacked."

"Attacked? What the hell?"

"Utes. They came at me in the night, no doubt after the horses, our supplies. The poor miserable bastards must be starving. But I killed them, saved us once again."

"You're a good man," breathed Newhart, and gripped his friend's arm. "And a damn fine friend."

"Well, thank-ee, Newhart, but I'm afraid one of them savages got away, which means..." He took in a long breath. "They'll be coming back, and then some. We have to get out of here, as quick as we can."

Newhart rolled his shoulders and gingerly touched his leg. "Damn if those fine people didn't patch me up good."

"Yes, they did. Fine people, as you say." And Mason looked away, not wanting Newhart to catch any hint in his eyes as to what had befallen his saviors.

Sixteen

The boat rolled slightly and Simms, unused to such movement, found himself having to hold onto the edge of the table as Ives poured out two healthy measures of whisky. He slid one across the tabletop and motioned for Simms to sit. Across from him, Ives unfolded the delivered message and considered the words quietly for a few moments. When he'd finished, he put the letter down and took a large mouthful of his drink.

"This is not good news," he said, staring into the bottom of his glass as he rolled it between his palms. "They want me to take on board troops, transport them up river to outflank the Mormons."

Simms didn't know what to say, so he sat and waited, watching Ives becoming more agitated, fingernails rapping on the glass, his mouth like a cow's, ruminating.

Ives spoke as if to himself, his voice trembling. "They have no idea what it's like here, exposed, working with poor equipment, with unqualified personnel, waiting, waiting for supplies, new orders. I'm supposed to be surveying the river, mapping it. We've barely begun… And now this." He waved the despatch, his face coming up and Simms noted the haunted look, the desperation, perhaps even fear. "What am I supposed to do if there's a war, huh? If hostilities break out? I'm not a fighter, Detective. I've never even fired my guns."

"You looked as though you would when we first arrived."

"Looks can be deceiving." Ives thrust his chair back and stood up, going over to the collection of bottles arrayed on another, smaller table. He filled his glass. "The Nauvoo Legion, you heard of them?" Simms shook his head. "Well, they're Mormon militia and they roam around these here parts. If they get wind of this plan, they'll launch a pre-emptive attack, burn my boat." He drank. Simms watched, silent. "They've been recruiting Indians, lots of them. They've given them food, the promise of salvation."

"In return for fighting on their behalf, I shouldn't wonder. We came across evidence of it, Lieutenant. More than once."

"You see, it's true. I always knew it." He drank, and as if by their own volition, his hands curled around the bottle and he poured himself another, bigger measure.

"We found a burnt out homestead, the adults killed, children, if there were any, gone. We buried them, as best we could." Simms took a sip of his own whisky. "We found the remains of soldiers, too. Colonel Johnston over at Bridger sent out two groups of troops to deliver that message previously. We ain't found the second, but I'm guessing they ended up like the first. Killed by Utes. We ran into some of them. It wasn't pretty."

"You done this sort of thing before? Fighting Indians, I mean?"

"I fought just about everybody there is, Lieutenant. I fought in the Mexican War, saw a lot of bad things. *Did* a lot of bad things. We had to. Mexicans don't take prisoners, if you get my meaning."

The glass rattled against his teeth as Ives took a mouthful before collapsing into his chair. "I don't think I can do this." He jabbed at the message with his forefinger. "When do these troops arrive?"

"As soon as I get back to Johnston, tell him the situation. Less than a fortnight I would guess."

"And what if the Mormons do get wind of this?" he said. "What if they launch an attack? I have twelve men here, Detective."

Simms nodded. "As I said, they were other messages sent. The men who were bringing them, they died so it's safe to assume the Mormons already know what the plan is. If they have any sense, they'll make their play sooner rather than later."

"What the hell does that mean?"

"It means, I suggest you make your defenses tight, Lieutenant, because they'll be coming this way. And when they do, people are going to die."

Ives gaped at the Pinkerton, slowly brought the glass to his lips, realized it was empty, and put it back down on the tabletop. "I don't even know why we're fighting them."

"Nor me. Land, suspicion, resentment... fear. Who knows? Brigham Young has upset Washington and that's all that matters. The country is breaking up, Lieutenant. I saw it during the war. Even though the fight was for sovereignty and the extension of the Union, I recognized the signs. A lot of people do not wish to be told what to do by a government which appears detached and ignorant. I think there's going to be a huge explosion of discontentment, and this Mormon thing, it's only the beginning. What we need is someone in charge who offers us all hope, who can help people live a good, wholesome life, without favor. Ordinary people, the backbone of our land, they need something to believe in."

"You'd make a good politician yourself, Detective."

Simms sniggered. "No, thank you! This is the only politics I understand," he patted the butt of the Colt Dragoon resting on his belt before he smiled and drained his glass. He sighed, reached inside his coat and brought out a torn, well-creased paper which he carefully smoothed out and placed in front of Ives, who frowned at it.

"What's this?"

"It's a wanted poster," said Simms. He leaned forward and tapped the amateurish drawings of two men. "These men are wanted for murder and kidnapping."

"Kidnapping? I don't understand. Why are you showing me this?"

"Because they are somewhere in the Territory. They're the real reason I'm here, Lieutenant. I've discharged Johnston's orders, delivered the message to you, now it's time to get back to my own business.

These men," he tapped their faces again, "they kidnapped the daughter of General Russell. You may not have heard of him, but he is highly regarded back east, and it's my job to find the girl and bring her home. These two are responsible. Newhart and Mason. I aim to bring them in to face justice, or kill them if circumstances call for it. I want you to remember these men, Lieutenant, and if they come this way, I want you to detain them and get a message to me at Fort Bridger."

"They don't look much."

"They are, believe you me." He took up the poster again, refolded it and slipped it into an inside pocket of his coat. "They are dangerous men, Lieutenant. Don't underestimate them."

"So, not only do you want me to make a stand here against the Nauvoo Legion, you want me to arrest and detain two desperados."

"That's about the size of it."

"You're all heart."

"For the time being, you need to post pickets, to keep an eye out for the enemy's approach."

"Yes, yes I shall. I will draft you a reply to this message," said Ives, setting his mouth into a thin line. "My surveying work must take precedence, and in a matter of weeks, the weather will change. It may not seem that way right now, but this drought will break and then winter will arrive. Nothing moves in the winter, not out here. It is my thinking that it would be best to delay the movement of troops here to the Colorado until the spring thaw."

"That's quite some way off, Lieutenant. I'm not at all sure Johnston would agree. He wants this situation addressed sooner, rather than later."

"Nevertheless, he cannot battle against nature. The wisest strategy would be to wait. I shall make this plain in the letter I wish you to take to him. In the meantime, we will prepare ourselves in case the Mormons launch an attack."

"You need to prepare well, Lieutenant. You can't sit here like a tethered goat, waiting for the mountain lion to come eat you all up. For the lion is coming, Lieutenant, believe you me." He stood up. "And he is mighty hungry."

* * *

He found Hanson fast asleep on the deck, with Landers sitting next to him, running a piece of bread around the inside of a bowl. The soldier raised his hand in welcome when Simms stepped up beside him and asked, "Have you eaten?" Simms shook his head. "Well, you should. The cook here makes our own seem like an amateur." He popped the last morsel into his mouth and stretched out his limbs. "How long we staying?"

"You're staying until the rest of the troop arrive. A week, or thereabouts."

Landers smiled. "That's music to my ears, Mister Simms. After what we've seen these past few days, I don't think I could take another ride through this miserable land."

Simms grunted and went across to the side railings. He peered down at the water gently lapping against the vessel's hull. He breathed in the air. "I could get used to this." He turned, leaning his back against the rail and studied the boat. The wheelhouse and upper deck were deserted, the long funnel positioned directly behind where the pilot would turn the wheel, its blackness in stark contrast to the gleaming white of the rest of the vessel. Towards the stern, the great paddles rested on the surface of the river, waiting patiently to churn into action. When that action might be, Simms did not know. In happier times, passengers would promenade along the decks, taking in the sunshine, enjoying long, leisurely days without worries. A few men wandered here and there right now, but other than that, it was a peaceful scene, almost as if taken from a poster advertising such lazy days on the river, an adventure of quiet and relaxation. *What's heading this way will be no vacation for anyone.* Simms shook his head. "I reckon no more than two hundred men could be carried on this boat," he said. "I wonder if that might be enough."

Landers lay back on the wooden deck, arms behind his head, eyes closed. "I'm sure it will be. Once them Mormons learn of our coming, they'll skedaddle back to where they came from and sign any goddamned treaty the army puts their way."

"You think so?"

"Of course. They ain't nothing but a bunch of ignorant farmers, preaching yet another story about God." He opened his eyes and peered up towards Simms. "I've met their like before, watched them in my hometown piling up their wagons, shouting out to us that Judgement Day was coming, that we should all 'prepare yee the way of the Lord'. We cheered when they finally left, damned bible-bashers." He sighed and sat up, rubbing his scalp with his fingers. "The way I see it, the sooner we pacify these people, the sooner we can get to making this country into something great. We need jobs, prosperity, security. It's the same with the Indians. We need to clear them out, make this a safe land in which to bring up our children."

"It's their land, or have you forgotten that?"

"Shit, I ain't forgot nothing! But look what they do, goddamn it! Look what they did to those people back at that homestead. What is that, defending their own, or just cold-blooded murder?"

"I reckon we've done greater harm to them than they will ever do to us. We're stealing their land. We don't negotiate, we don't talk, we just take. Where's the sense in that?"

"You sound like one of them bony-assed liberals, living in some ivory tower, saying we should all live in peace and understanding. It's bullshit."

"Well, I think it's a might easier to live alongside one another and try to get along, than to kill each other over a piece of dirt."

"Well, once they're all dead, we won't have any more worries, will we?"

Simms sighed. "Once they're all dead… And what happens if we're the ones who are all dead? How many people have to die before you can sleep safe in your bed at night? I've seen death, Landers. Killing. Rape, pillage, suffering. I've watched children wailing over the bodies of their dead parents, parents who believed all they need do was stand and shoot. Killing, all it does is make people kill more."

"But you've killed." Landers nodded towards Simms's coat. "I've seen that wanted poster you carry with you. You're gonna kill those men, ain't you? For what they did?"

"If needs be."

"Well shit, you're no better than any of us. You're a hypocrite, that's what you is. Standing there with your fancy words about peace and understanding, jeez, you'd kill those two mangy curs as soon as spit."

"I reckon that's about right."

"So all what you said, that's just words."

"No. There's a difference between those who are forced to kill, to preserve their way of life, and cold-hearted killers who take lives for the love of it."

"I don't see the difference. You know as well as I do, we have to rid this land of the evil that dwells within it. Indians, fanatics, people like those you're after. There is no other way. If they ain't willing to give up and accept the inevitable, we have to crush them like the bugs they are."

"All bugs ain't bad."

"No, but they're all ugly." Landers sniggered. "Damn it, mister, we can't let them bastards get in the way of what is right. If they won't listen to reason, then they have to be swept away. It's that simple."

Simms chewed at his lip, took a last glance towards the river, and stared into its depths for several moments. "Well, it's a sorry state, that's for sure. I'm not sure how it will end, but a lot of good people will die in the process."

"A lot of bad ones too."

"I don't believe Indians are *bad*. They're doing what we'd all do if we were under attack – they defend themselves, that's all."

"Yeah, well let's hope it's over real quick."

"Yeah. Let's hope."

He tipped his hat and walked across the deck to the gangplank.

Simms left the boat later the same day, cutting across the prairie the way he had come, but choosing to skirt around the scenes of death he'd encountered previously. He made good going and knew nothing of what was to befall Lieutenant Ives and the others back at the boat.

Seventeen

A ragged trail of over forty riders meandered across the open prairie, outriders ahead. Interspersed along the line were covered wagons, four in total, and the clatter of pans and cooking utensils rang out over the range, signaling their approach. Mason, lying flat on the ridge of a hill, pondered what to do as he watched the procession slowly moving forward.

He rolled over and scrambled down to his own waiting wagon. Newhart was on the buckboard, round-shouldered, still not his former self. He raised his head slightly as Mason came up to him.

"They ain't soldiers, but there's enough of them to say they're out for a fight."

Newhart frowned. "Indians?"

"No. Not sure who or what they are. They don't seem like normal settlers. Mainly men, armed. I could see their rifles. Some women are amongst them, but not many. No sign of any children, so I'm thinking they're some sort of militia."

"Militia? What the hell is that?"

"Like a private army, I guess. With so many guns, it stands to reason they're preparing to fight."

"What do you think we should do?"

Mason shrugged and rubbed his grizzled chin. "Beats me. We could go the opposite way, but we need supplies, Newhart. Water. Water more than anything else. We've got a day or two left, I reckon, before we keel over and die."

"Oh, well that's just dandy." Newhart turned away and put his face in his hands. "We should never have come out here, Mason. God-damn it, we should have stayed at the goldmine, tried harder, made a go of it." He threw his head back. "Oh dear God Almighty, we never meant to fall in with scoundrels, thieves and murderers!" He brought both his fists down on either side of himself, pounding the buckboard. "We're being punished, that's what this is, Mason, punished for all the bad things we done."

"Stop with that fucking whining." Mason hawked and spat. "We ain't being punished, not by no god, nor devil or any such thing. We's here because we is here, and that's that. We had no choice, Newhart, no choice at all. There never was no fucking gold."

"We weren't to know that."

"We stayed too long and that's the truth of it, and here we are. No point in crying over what should have been. We made our own play then and we make our own play now, so we have to join them." He jerked his thumb towards the hill beyond.

"*Join* them?" Newhart lifted his head. "Are you crazy? Militia you said, a private army you said! What if they're the law, Mason, or they have a U.S. Marshall with them? What if they recognize us and hang us from the nearest tree?"

"There ain't no trees, Newhart."

Newhart's face grew red with rage. "You know what the fuck I mean! Holy God, Mason, you could be leading us to our deaths."

"Well, we're staring right into our graves if we sit here, or ride off in the other direction. You don't seem to understand – *we ain't got no supplies*! We must do what we must do, so we join them."

"And what if they recognize us? All the things we've done, shit, we must be wanted all across the Territory."

"We play it out, Newhart, we make as if we're somebody else, that's all."

"And lie, you mean?" Mason nodded. "We have to get our story straight, because if we don't, we'll be dead."

"We tell them we're on the run from Indians, who attacked our settlement. They'll swallow that. It's happening all around these parts. And besides, it's almost the truth."

"And if they don't believe us? What happens if one of them has a wanted poster with our faces on it?"

"Then we shoot our way out, as we've always done. You're feeling better now, so we can do it. We take what we can and get the hell away."

"Where to? Damn it, I don't know, Mason. We seem to be just drifting. We have no purpose anymore."

"Purpose? Like teaming up with those ingrates we met back at the mine and robbing that bank?"

"We took the girl. We should have ransomed her, got some money together, made something of our lives. Here, we're just like prairie dogs, scratching out whatever we can."

Mason blew out his cheeks. "We could always go back and take her again."

Newhart spluttered, words catching in his throat, and he fell into a bout of violent coughing. Mason watched him in silence. When the coughing stopped, Mason took a breath. "You finished now?"

Newhart shook his head, eyes streaming and he reached for his neckerchief, pulled it loose and dabbed at his face. "Shit, Mason, are you out of your mind? We can't go back there; they'll shoot us stone dead."

"Well, there you have it, you fucking whining idiot! We can't go back and we can't sit here, so we have to join those riders. Whoever they are. So pull yourself together, check your weapons, and haul on out!"

In a little over thirty minutes, Newhart steered the wagon around the hillside and along a well-worn pathway which brought them back out onto the plain. Mason rode on the horse, a little way off, keeping to the high ground, with the procession of riders always in sight. As soon as Newhart made level ground and the dust rose up in clouds from the wheels, the outriders spotted their approach, wheeled their mounts and came forward in a tight knot. Half a dozen or so men, grim-faced and alert. Mason reined in his horse, looking beyond the approaching group to check the far horizon for others. He didn't want to be ambushed or outflanked. When he was confident there were no other armed men heading their way, he took his horse down the slight incline and came up alongside the wagon. He looked at Newhart and winked. Newhart grimaced as if he were in pain.

The sound of the approaching horses caused them to both turn and face them.

Mason remained relaxed and when the riders reined in, horses blowing out their breath in loud snorts, nobody spoke for a long time, measuring one another, waiting. The pressure mounted, the air between them crackling with tension.

Finally, one of the riders leaned forward in his saddle, the leather creaking, and smiled. "Friends. Can I ask you why you're shadowing us?"

Mason, without a pause, returned the lazy smile. "We need your help."

The lead rider frowned, clearly not expecting this response. "Well, you certainly do look as if you are in *need* of assistance, but I'm not sure what we could do for you, friend."

"Some water. Food maybe. My friend here," he gestured to Newhart who sat rigid, expression locked in terror, "he's been shot by Indians. We were lucky to get away with our lives. I'm sorry I cannot say the same for our families."

The rider's frown deepened. "Indians? When was this?"

"*Where* was this," interjected a second rider.

"Two or three days' ride from here, to the east. We've been on the trail ever since, heading for the river. But our water has gone. If it is only water you could give us, you would be saving our lives."

The lead rider straightened and glanced sideways to the second. The slightest shrugging of shoulders. A drawn out moment of contemplation.

"Very well," said the lead rider at last. "You can follow us, but you put all your firearms in the back of the wagon. Any nonsense from either of you two gentlemen…" He smiled. "Well, I'm sure we don't have to spell anything out to you."

He moved to turn his horse away when Newhart suddenly shouted out, "Who are you people?"

They stopped, and the leader rider swiveled in his saddle. "We're a detachment of the Nauvoo Legion, and we're on our way to meet our destiny at the Colorado River."

And when they cantered away, Mason let out a long, silent whistle and turned to his friend. "We've just either hit the jackpot, or… signed away our lives."

Newhart blinked a number of times, then slumped back in his seat and groaned.

Eighteen

Three of them came from out of the shimmering heat, one astride a pony, pulling a sled. On this lay the second man, inert, eyes rolling in his head – eyes which, when Elisabeth first saw them, she recognized as holding the look of someone close to death. It reminded her of the look her father gave her before Mason bundled her into the wagon. And as she stepped down from the porch and bent over to study this stricken man, thoughts of her father loomed up in her mind and she wondered if he died that day. For a moment, she could not speak, the memory too powerful, too distressing.

Behind the sled stood a woman, very beautiful, with huge, black eyes, dark blue hair scraped back from her olive skinned, oval-shaped face. A fierce expression, one of pride and bravery, caught Elisabeth's full attention and when she tried a smile the girl did not respond.

"We need food," said the man on the pony in English. He slid down to the ground. Small, wiry, his body a museum of deprivations. Old before his time, eyes sunk in a face etched with lines of worry, hunger, thirst. Elisabeth had never seen a native this close. She always expected them to be proud, strong, bodies hewn out of teak. Not like this. "If you can spare some."

Elisabeth glanced back to the other members of the family assembled around the entrance to the house, guns in their hands. They all nodded in unison and Elisabeth led the man to the barn where he tied up the pony. Elisabeth fetched water and grain and as the pony refreshed itself, she beckoned for the man and woman to enter the house, "There's food already inside," she said. The man nodded his thanks, and together with the girl, went into the house.

Elisabeth stooped and studied the other man on the sled. He was old and grey, his breathing shallow and from his stick-thin body rose an acrid smell, one of sickness and decay. They must have walked miles, this sorry trio of humanity, exposed to the relentless sun, with little or no water. From a bucket, she soaked an old rag, wrung it out, and dabbed it across the old man's lips. He responded, head lolling, eyes flickering. She squeezed the cloth to allow a few drops to fall into the crusted black hole of a mouth. He moaned, so low.

The sun dipped down below the horizon and she stayed with him, out in the open, afraid to move him lest his body crumble like a withered, dried up old tree. She stayed with him until the night came on, and the old man's companions emerged from the house, transformed, a new light in their eyes.

A light, which died as the old man too died.

They made a burial pyre and they all gathered in the silence to watch the body burn. The other man gave up a sing-song prayer, face lifted skywards, and his woman quietly sobbed.

Later, the two strangers slept in the barn with their pony.

Around the table before they retired to their beds, Elisabeth rested her chin on her hands and stared into nothingness, two flickering candles giving off a faint light, casting everyone's faces in grotesque shadows. "What will become of them?"

"I've heard it said," said Sarah, "that men out of Fort Bridger and Laramie are buying up parcels of land from the Indians, giving them firearms and whisky in return. Dispossessed, these poor people make their way further into the west in the hope of finding new land where they might scrape out a life." She shook her head, looking to the others who all remained tight-lipped, reflective. "But, of course, that new life is a fallacy. This is the longest drought we have ever known. The land is scorched and barren. There is no 'new life', it is all a lie. These wicked, sinful men dispossess these people, sewing seeds of discontent and that is why the troubles began."

"And now the Government intervenes," put in Jacob, leaning back in his chair, "taking the side of these men because they are powerful, men of influence. Cattle men, bringing their herds of beef to roam across the prairies, prairies that once were filled with buffalo."

Sarah nodded. "We have befriended the native people from these parts, the Utes. They are good people, but quick to violence if they feel threatened. Some have embraced our beliefs, others have not, choosing to remain on the range, to fight if need be."

"And the two in the barn?" asked Elisabeth. "What of them?"

"Dispossessed," said Jacob. "Driven from their homes, their land, no doubt coerced, promises of new beginnings, all of that. But this region is unforgiving and their suffering is evident. I fear for them if they continue on their journey, but I'm fearful also that they may wish to do so, despite the dangers."

Elisabeth sighed. "Could they not stay here? We have room, and they could help us with the fields. We need to dig out irrigation ditches and–"

"We will ask them," said Sarah, "and if Our Heavenly Father wishes it so, then they will stay. But… I am not sure. I believe their destiny lies to the west."

And the following morning, Elisabeth found them both already making their preparations to leave. Before she could speak, the girl came to her, took Elisabeth's hands in hers and squeezed them. She smiled, tipped her head and said, "Thank you."

Sarah stepped out from the house with two bundles of food and a canteen of water. "Make for the river and follow its course," she said to them both. "Replenish your supplies whenever you can." She glanced upwards. "I pray for rain. We all do."

The two women stood and watched the couple move away, the man on the pony, pulling the sled. Behind, the woman. Resolute, no questions asked, a simple, grim acceptance of their destiny.

When they were nothing more than tiny black smudges in the distance, Sarah took Elisabeth's hand. "You are blessed, Elisabeth. You tended to them without hesitation or fear. I believe you are already one of us, without you even knowing."

Elisabeth smiled, but deep in her heart, she knew she could not stay in that place for much longer. The memory of her father brought with it a strong desire to find him, to discover if he still lived and if he did, to bring to him once more the joy of being together.

Nineteen

Simms's changed route took him into an area he knew little about and he wished he had brought either Hanson or Landers with him. They had billeted in this land long enough to be aware of the various settlements and townships which were springing up all over the Territory. When he reached a ridge, he pulled out the telescope Hanson supplied and scanned the wide basin, which spread out beneath him. Nestling amongst the ash and scrub stood a small scattering of buildings, which may, or may not, be termed a town. A larger area of flat ground ran slightly to the east, broader and greener, dotted with tiny shapes. Cattle. Simms sighed, snapped the eyepiece shut and slowly steered his horse down the hill, towards the buildings.

He padded along the street, a quiet, grim place, the buildings featureless, some not yet painted, bare wooden panels buckling in the heat. Somewhere far off a dog barked, but other than this, there was little sign of life and Simms began to wonder if this could be a ghost town, as rapidly deserted as it was erected. But then he remembered the cattle and he dismissed this notion. People lived here, they simply did not venture out.

He reined in his horse outside the grandest of the buildings and went up to the main door. He knocked and entered.

It was a wide, dark room, with desks down both sides creating a walkway through the center. But no one was here and his voice, when he raised a single, "Hello!" echoed back to him and he knew at once it was empty.

Outside once more, he stood on the veranda, scanned the street and took in a deep breath. There was a bank, two stores, a hotel-cum-saloon, a telegraph office and various other buildings without signs. All appeared lifeless. Nevertheless, he needed supplies, a place to rest up, so he crossed the street to the hotel and went through the door.

At a semi-circular desk, a man bent over a large ledger, scribbling furiously with a stubby pencil. He was dressed in black satin waist coat and white shirt, stained with sweat, and on the top of his head were perched his spectacles, pushed back to allow him to peer at the ledger from a short distance. When Simms entered he stopped, half-raised his head, and gave a grimace. "You've missed it."

Simms took a moment, taking his eyes from the various tables and chairs, all covered with a fine film of dust, and frowned. "Missed what?"

"The funeral. You from Iowa?"

"Why the hell would I be from Iowa?"

The man straightened up. Slightly built, he nevertheless wore the demeanor of a man quick to temper, unfriendly and suspicious. "I'll let your surly tone pass for now, stranger. I myself hail from Iowa, as gracious a state as any in this fair Union."

"Well, be that as it may, I am not from there, but from Illinois. Chicago to be exact."

"*Chicago*? Well, good God Almighty. What in the name of all that is holy are you doing all the way out here?"

Simms stepped up to the counter and slowly took off his hat. "I'm on my way over to Fort Bridger, to deliver a message to the commanding officer there."

"Shoot," said the man. "Didn't you know? Bridger was burned down, by God. There can't be anything there now."

"There's an army camp. I know that much as I left it a few days back. No doubt they'll get round to rebuilding the fort once these hostilities are ended."

"Hostilities? We've had enough of those, I reckon." He cocked his head. "So, you ain't here for the funeral?"

"Nope, just passing through. Thought I might take some rest here before I continue tomorrow."

"Well, we have an abundance of rooms. The entire place will be shipping out over the next few weeks I shouldn't wonder, now that Pilcher is gone."

"Pilcher?"

"He owned the ranch here, brought in a lot of money for the town. He was making a go of it too, before those two bastards rode in here and changed everything for us."

The blood ran cold in Simms's veins. He stared, unblinking at the man, his voice ice when he spoke. "Two men? Villainous men?"

"I reckon they was spawned from the Devil himself. They came here to receive attention for some wounds they had received and when confronted, they shot and killed old man Pilcher. Then the big one, he came down this street and I saw it, bold as day. He shot Pilcher's four best men, shot them dead. Then that bastard went back to poor Doctor Ned's and shot him and his sister too." He lowered his head. "She's in a wheelchair, bless her heart. Got a bullet in the brain, so they say. She can't talk, needs help with her eating, her toilet and the like. She'd be better off dead if you ask me."

Simms pulled out the wanted poster and laid it down very carefully in front of the man. "These two?"

"Dear God Almighty." The man's eyes filled with tears. "Are you on their trail, because if you are, you are a better man than any here. No one had the balls to go after them. I'm ashamed to say it, but neither have I."

"Don't fret none," said Simms and refolded the poster. "They're merciless killers, been shooting their way across the Territory and I've a mind to bring them to justice. Dead or alive."

"I'd prefer them dead."

"I reckon most people would agree." His mouth broadened slightly into a humorless smile. "Me too." He picked up his hat and placed it back on his head, straightening the brim with a flourish. "I'll have a room, with a bath." He snapped a silver dollar on the counter. "Have it ready as I'll be away for no more than an hour."

"Where you going?"

"To see the girl. The sister of the doctor."

"She doesn't make much sense, slips in and out if you understand me. There is a doctor coming, from Salt Lake, but God alone knows when he will get here. Her name is Cathy. A lovely girl she was, but now…"

Simms grunted and went out into the sunlight.

* * *

Cathy sat in the wheelchair, head drooping, eyes closed. She did not stir as Simms came into the house, the front door wide open allowing whatever breeze there might be to make some impression on the stifling heat.

A stout woman came out of a side room and she held a rifle. Simms raised both arms. "I'm friendly, ma'am."

"I doubt that," she snapped, levelling the rifle towards Simms's chest. "Or might you be the doctor out of Salt Lake?"

"No, ma'am. I'm here to ask the young lady something."

"Well, she ain't up to talking." She jerked her head towards Cathy, who continued to sleep. "She rarely talks anymore at all."

"Because of the bullet?"

The woman scowled. "Who the hell are you?"

"Name is Simms. I'm a Detective out of Chicago, Illinois, and I'm here to put the bastards that did this in the ground."

The woman reeled with this news and slowly lowered the rifle. Her eyes, however, remained hostile. "A detective?"

"Yes ma'am. We're known as Pinkerton's. I was sent to find the daughter of a general, kidnapped by the same two scoundrels that shot this here poor girl."

"They went north."

Both Simms and the woman turned in surprise towards Cathy, who had lifted her head. Her mouth seemed as if pulled down from one corner by an invisible string, the eye above it also drooping, half closed. Her other eye, however, shone bright and alert and Simms saw within it the memory of her loveliness. "Please don't stress yourself, Cathy," said the women and went to her side, patting the hand which gripped the arm of the wheelchair.

Simms stepped closer, pulling off his hat. "Miss, my apologies if I woke you. I do not wish to cause you distress, but if you can tell me anything about the men that did this, I would be grateful."

"The bullet is in her head," said the woman with a snap, bending down next to Cathy, stroking the girl's hand. "We must keep her quiet until the doctor arrives and tends to her."

Simms nodded, his eyes never leaving the girl. Despite one side of her face being frozen in an aspect of lifelessness, her other side continued to radiate, clear and wholesome and as he gazed, something buried deep stirred inside Simms. He swallowed hard, throat suddenly dry. "North, you said?"

She nodded. Her voice, when it came, was soft but slurred, the words rolling into one, the lips on her lifeless side thick, unresponsive. "They mentioned a ferry."

"Dear Christ," breathed Simms.

Later, back at the hotel, after a long soak in a hot bath, Simms dined on steak with green beans, and drank a thin, almost tasteless beer. He retired to his simple room and fell into a fitful sleep, his Colt Dragoon forever at his side, the images of the men he would kill imprinted on his mind. For now, he knew they must die, to end the scourge which they brought to everyone's lives they encountered. His remit was to find Elisabeth Randall, bring her home if need be, but now another course was laid out straight before him. For everyone's sake, but especially for Cathy and the suffering she endured.

Newhart and Mason must die.

Twenty

They eased their way into the makeshift camp, conscious of the eyes boring into them. Mason, aware of the many guns, made sure his hands hung loose at his side. Forty or more gun hands were not the sort of odds he ever wanted to face.

The man standing before him was slight, black hair set in a rolling wave shape across his head, a thick growth of beard covering his neck only, the remainder of his face clean-shaven, lending him an almost Biblical air. His eyes gleamed with an intensity Mason had rarely seen. With his feet planted wide apart, hands on hips, this man appeared tense, ready to spring into action and despite him not wearing a gun, Mason decided, almost at once, that if trouble broke out, this man would be the first to die.

In an attempt to relieve the tension, Mason smiled, tipping his hat. "Thank you for allowing us into your camp. It's mighty kind of you."

The man's voice came back hard, low and even. "We always do our best to help fellow travelers."

Mason nodded, looking askance at Newhart, who appeared unusually agitated, sweating profusely, lips quivering. "My friend is recovering from a fever. Hence him seeming all nervous and all."

"I see."

But Mason noted the man took no real interest, his air of detached indifference unsettling. "We were set upon by Indians."

A slight flickering of interest. "Bannock People?"

Mason frowned. "I ain't got no clue what they called themselves, but they was murdering sons of whores and I killed three of them, but not before they killed our family and left my friend here for dead."

The rider who first met Mason shifted his weight, thumbs hooked under his gun belt. "Best for you to refrain from such language, friend. We don't abide no cussing here."

Mason nodded, storing away the comment for future reference. He looked around the assembled gathering, mainly men, along with a few women who from a distance or perhaps even close up, he would have taken for men anyway. They were a hardy, weather-beaten bunch and they appeared single-minded, determined. For what, Mason could not guess. "My apologies," said Mason. "We've been on the trail for too long, I'm guessing, and the loss of loved ones has turned me somewhat vengeful."

"Such things are common out here," said the strangely-bearded man. "My name is Jacob Hamblin. I am a minister sent by Our Heavenly Father to bring His divine teachings to the native peoples of this land. I am shocked to hear you speak thus about them. We are all God's creatures, my friend. There are always reasons why people do what they do."

"Well..." Mason chewed on his lip, scanning the band all around, aware of a smoldering hostility. He knew he would need to be cautious in the extreme. "Like I say, apologies for sounding so belligerent. Circumstance makes me so."

Hamblin nodded. "Understandable." He looked towards the lead rider. "Brother Skinner, take these poor unfortunates to eat supper and take water. Tend to their animals also, for they seem in dire need of refreshment. When done, bring this good gentleman to my tent." Then, without a further word, he turned on his heels and went back towards the rest of his companions, who gathered around him, muttering together in low tones.

Skinner, the lead rider, stepped up close, his eyes burning. "I did ask for you to leave your guns in the wagon."

Mason's mouth formed a round 'o' before he smiled and slowly pulled back his coat. "I forgot."

Skinner reached forward, took Mason's Navy Colt without a word, and handed it over to one of the others close by. "You get it back when you leave."

"Thank you kindly."

Skinner's eyes remained flat, unemotional. "We'll fix you something to eat, provide you with water. Tomorrow, you can be on your way."

Mason smiled, looked across to Newhart whose demeanor had not yet changed, and grinned. "Well, isn't that just dandy, Newhart?"

"Fine and," said Newhart quietly. Skinner's eyes never flickered as he went to Newhart and relieved him of his six-gun. He studied both men for a moment before turning. Both fell in behind him and he led them to where a fire with cooking pots settled on top awaited them.

They ate in silence, some of the others sitting a few paces away, shooting across the occasional glance, full of wariness. Newhart dipped bread into his broth and muttered out the corner of his mouth, eyes down, voice low, "They keep staring."

"Just eat," said Mason. "We'll fill our bellies, get some water and get the hell out."

"Who are they?"

"I don't know. I might know more after I've spoken to that Hamblin guy."

"He seems mean, Mason. What should I do if you don't return from your meeting?"

Mason sniggered, munched down a piece of bread, and arched a single eyebrow in Newhart's direction. "Then you take as many of them with you before they blow your brains out." Then he belched loudly and ignored the looks of disgust from the others seated close by.

In his tent, Hamblin sat on a canvas chair, right leg over left forming a sort of table for the large book he settled across his knees. He looked up as Mason came through the flap, with Skinner close behind.

"I have no other chair, my friend."

"That's of no consequence, Mr. Hamblin," said Mason. "I'm used to standing."

"And what else might you be *used to*, my friend?"

"I don't get your meaning."

"Well, what I mean is, forgive me for coming straight to the point, but you ain't no family man, friend."

Mason grinned, shot a glance at Skinner whose hands hovered close to the gun at his hip. "I ain't your friend either."

"No, I did not think so." Hamblin closed the large book and placed it on the ground with a great deal of care. He uncrossed his legs and leaned forward, elbows on knees. "Are you army men?"

"Army? Hell no."

Skinner coughed and Mason gave him a glance. "Sorry. No cussing. I forgot. But no, I ain't Army. Why, you expecting them?"

"We are indeed. My ministry is with the natives. I preach the Book, offering salvation, peace and understanding. But the Army, if and when it comes, threatens all of that. If your story is true—"

"It is."

Hamblin nodded. "Then already the Indians are reacting in the way they know best. If the Bannocks, Shoshone and the Utes rise up, there could be fearful times ahead. No one will be safe out on this prairie."

"But why is the Army coming?"

"To face us down. I am at the head of a scouting party, whilst behind me, at Echo Canyon, we prepare to defend what is ours. You, my friend, have wandered into a war zone."

"Then I'd best make my way out of it."

"I would recommend you do so, as soon as dawn rises. We will give you supplies, enough for your journey to the south."

"South? We was heading north, to the ferry at the Colorado."

"There are soldiers at the ferry," put in Skinner. "We may be forced to confront them."

Mason grew eager, mind racing through the opportunities such an action might bring. Food, money, a means to get away. "We could help, Newhart and me. We wouldn't let you down."

"Oh, I'm sure of that," said Hamblin, "but no, I do not think we have need of your services, friend."

"My name's Mason."

"Yes. Of course." Hamblin sighed and leaned back in his chair. "But thank you anyway, Mr. Mason. My advice would be for you to head south, towards the town of Bovey. It's an old mining town, a little rundown, but would suit you admirably."

"What do you mean by that, *friend?*"

He sensed Skinner stiffening behind him, imagining the man's hand curling around the grip of his revolver.

"I think you know." Hamblin smiled and stood up. "We are a God-fearing people, Mr. Mason, but we will always protect ourselves, come what may. You understand me?"

"Oh, I think I do, yes."

"Then we part with that understanding. I shall not see you in the morning. I hope I *never* see you again."

Mason nodded, swung around and left, punching aside the tent flap as he did so.

* * *

Skinner blew out his cheeks, allowing his shoulders to drop. He turned to face Hamblin. "We should string him up."

"Oh?" Hamblin lowered himself back into his chair and reached for the book. He opened it. "And pass over the opportunity of earning us some money?" He chuckled, licked a forefinger and turned a page. Carefully placed between the sheaves was a small poster, which he lifted and studied as if for the first time. "These sketches do not do them justice." Laughing still, he passed the wanted poster over to Skinner. "They are far uglier in real life."

Skinner's eyes roamed over the pictures of the two men. "Newhart and Mason. Murdering scoundrels is what they are. How did you know we'd cross their path?"

"I didn't. But they are notorious desperadoes, known throughout the Territory and when the opportunity presents itself, we must grasp it, with both hands."

"They seem unaware of their infamy."

"Ignorance, in their case, is certainly bliss."

"Like I say, we should string 'em up, right here. It'd save us a good deal of trouble."

"I do not want the women and young folk to witness such a thing."

"So, how do we handle it?"

"They're dangerous, especially Mason. We allow them to leave camp unmolested. You shadow them, without being seen, and when a suitable place for ambush presents itself, kill them. Long-range if possible. I have an inkling our friend Mason is particularly skilled with those pistols hc carries."

"I'm with you there. Then what?"

"Take the bodies back to Salt Lake, claim the bounty. Then buy guns, Skinner. As many as you can." His eyes returned to the book. "We need to prepare for war, Skinner. We must defend what is ours."

"And the ferry?"

Hamblin pulled out a second piece of paper from within the pages of the book. "If this message is true that our Ute friends gave us, and I see no reason to doubt its validity, we'll proceed to the ferry, put a hole in their riverboat, and put paid to their dastardly schemes to outflank us. They have underestimated us, Skinner. I do not plan to do the same with them."

Twenty-one

Johnston read Ives's letter, chomping on a large, unlit cigar whilst Simms sat opposite him in silence.

When he finished, Johnston rocked back in his chair and slowly pulled out a small metal box, out of which he produced a match. He struck it along the side of the box and it flared up. He touched the flame to the cigar. He puffed away for some considerable time, rolling the thick cigar from one corner of his mouth to the other before he took it from between his teeth and studied the glowing end.

"How did you find him?"

"Find him? I'm not sure I—"

"His demeanor. Was he confused, scatty, incoherent?"

"None of those things."

"Are you sure? This," he came forward, picked up the letter and wafted it in front of Simms, "was he in sound mind when he wrote it?"

"I believe so."

"Was he drunk, perhaps?"

"What are you getting at?"

"I don't know, but why the desire to stall, to postpone our advance?"

"He told you – the winter. Perhaps he knows something you don't; after all, he's been here longer."

Johnston's eyes narrowed and he took a long pull on the cigar. "Maybe… Or maybe he's met with those Latter Day Saints already? He's reached some form of agreement with them. I've received further communications from Washington. Word has reached the President that the Saints are pacifying Indians, bringing them to their cause. Perhaps they have done the same with Ives?"

"I saw no evidence of that."

"Mm..." Johnston blew out a long stream of acrid smoke. "Well, he may have a point, although I can't see this drought lifting for quite some time."

"When it does and the rains come, there could be flash-floods, the land turned into a quagmire. It happens fast."

"Now who's the local expert?"

Simms sighed heavily, his patience coming to its end. "Colonel, I couldn't give a tuppenny-damn if you move towards the Colorado now, or in four to five months. You do what you think best, all I need is directions to the ranch house you told me about. I've done my part of the bargain, now you do yours."

"And you are certain the bodies you found, they were—"

"I told you. We came across a family, and later on some soldiers. It is my belief any message you gave them was either taken or destroyed."

"But Utes can't read."

"Well then..." Simms spread out his hand. "If these Mormons are planning an attack, I doubt it's based on stolen information. Even if it were, you seriously think they would launch an attack?"

"I do, Detective. I surely do. I must prepare for all eventualities, so I shall send out a small task-force, led by Lieutenant Calhoon, to reinforce the ferry. We will then winter here before moving our main force along the Colorado. I can't afford Ives's command falling into the hands of the Saints."

"Well, all my best to you. For my own part, I have to find Elisabeth Randall, and the two men who kidnapped her. They've been bringing down a rain of hellfire right across the Territory. I mean to bring an end to it."

"Then we part with decisions made." He crossed over to the tent entrance and Simms followed him. They shook hands. "You'll be wanting those two recruits as well, I suppose."

"If you can spare them."

"It's the horses I can't spare, Detective. They'll take mules. I've given instructions and the Quartermaster has drawn up a map. Call in before you leave. I'd like to wish you well before you set off." He pulled hard on the cigar. "I keep my word, Detective, as I hope you realize."

"I do indeed, Colonel. Thank you. Your service will not go without mention when I deliver my report back at my headquarters. And to the General, too."

"He's still alive?"

"Yes, thank God. A telegram gave me the news I was hoping for, although by all accounts, he'll never be the same again. Which reminds me," he glanced away for a moment, images of Cathy sitting in the wheelchair, the dreadful contrast between the two sides of her face conjuring up a mix of emotions, "I have a lot of things to settle, Colonel. This land is not only brutal, it's full of surprises."

Johnston grunted. "Not all of them good, Detective."

"No. But some are." He brought his heels together, saluted and left.

He found Winterton polishing the brass buckles of his belt, stretched out in the sun, shirt soaked through with sweat. In the tent, asleep, lay Ableman, snoring.

"You got news?" asked Winterton, squinting towards Simms who stood, looking out to the west.

"Some. We're leaving at first light. You and Ableman are to get yourselves over to the Quartermaster. He'll give you equipment and supplies, and a map. You tell Ableman he'll need his wits about him on the range. This ain't going to be no tea-party."

Winterton grunted. "Shit, it's like I always knew… They told us, 'no fighting, boys'… lies, the whole damn lot of it."

"Yeah, well. They told you about your pay, which also didn't come to pass. If you help me, there'll be money in it for the both of you."

"Truly?"

"Absolutely. It may not be a fortune, but it'll be a damn sight more than you've ever seen before. Could buy you a new tailoring business."

Winterton's eyes widened. "Holy Mother, if that don't beat all!"

Simms smiled. "I'm riding out to go visit someone. I'll be back before daybreak. If I'm not, for any reason, you just wait."

Winterton watched him go, fell back against the canvas side of the tent and gave out a long, low whistle.

As things turned out, Simms journey was shorter than he expected. He rode into the crumbling town of Pilcher and the maid met him at the door. She seemed troubled, eyes wet and as soon as she saw him, she took Simms by the arm and guided him into the parlor. "She's taken bad, mister. *Real* bad."

Simms bit his lip. "Since when?"

"Yesterday morning. She woke up, bright and breezy, asking for some breakfast, and when I brought her the coffee…" Her body jerked with a great sob and she turned away, pressing a handkerchief to her nose and mouth. She fell into a small sofa. "She took a sip and it must have caught in her throat, for she took to the most awful coughing. Then her eyes rolled, the coffee cup fell from her fingers and she went into a dead faint. She's been that way ever since."

"The coughing must have caused the bullet to move."

"That's what I'm thinking. Dear God, do you think she can hold on until the doctor gets here?"

Simms held her gaze. "She has to. She has to."

He spent a few moments standing in the doorway of her bedroom, watching her. Her breathing was low and even, her pallor normal-looking. When he roused himself and went closer, he picked up her hand. It was warm, soft. She appeared as if in a deep sleep, but Simms knew it was far worse. The bandage around her head remained dry, with no blood having seeped through. That had to be a good thing, he told himself. How many men had he watched die slow, agonizing deaths from wounds, which turned green-black, tracing virulent trails through the skin, sending them into delirium, then death? Too many. He breathed through clenched teeth, squeezed her hand and left. With his head down, he almost bumped into the maid in the hallway. He gave a little jump, smiled a self-conscious apology.

The maid screwed up the handkerchief she held, her eyes full of concern. "How is she?"

"Sleeping. Listen, I'm going away for a few days, hopefully by the time I get back the doctor will have been. Do you know how deep the bullet is?"

"I could see it," she said, shaking her head. "It grazed her along the side of her skull, not penetrating all that far."

"She's mighty lucky. Once the damn thing is out, we might see some improvement." He thought for a moment, then reached inside his coat. He brought out his wallet and counted out several dollar bills.

The maid raised her eyebrows. "What's this?"

"For the doctor," said Simms and pressed the money into her hand. "Twenty-five dollars. I've been frugal, as I always am. If he requires more, tell him I will see him right when I return."

She must have caught a hint of his Pinkerton badge, for she reached out a finger and said, "Who are you mister?"

"I'm a detective," he slapped the wallet shut and put it back inside his coat. "I'm here on business, to apprehend two men. The two men who did this."

"But why you helping? With the money and all?"

Simms smiled and shrugged. He felt his cheeks warm up, "Oh, you know…"

She returned his smile. "Yes. Yes, I think I do."

He tipped his hat and went out.

It was night by the time he returned to the tented camp outside the remains of Fort Bridger. The guards waved him through without a word and when he found the tent, Ableman was again asleep. Winterton was sitting outside, smoking a cigarette.

"You get everything?" asked Simms, putting some of his belongings inside the tent before he stepped outside again to take in the night air.

"We got guns, food, water, bed-rolls and the map. We're heading north-east, about two day's ride, or so the Quartermaster says. Apparently it's well-known, this place we're going to. A ranch. Protected, or so he said."

"Protected? Who by?"

Winterton chuckled and smoked his cigarette for a moment. "By God."

Twenty-two

It was during the late afternoon of the next day that Mason reined in his horse, swung her around and wandered back to the wagon. Newhart stopped, took the chance to unstop his canteen to drink, then shot a questioning look at his friend as he came up alongside.

"Problem?"

Mason grinned, blew out a breath and turned his face to the sky. "Some. But don't you let it trouble you, just keep following. We'll camp soon, then we'll talk."

"What the hell are you talking about, Mason? Have we got trouble or not?"

Mason lowered his head, shrugged, the grin set like a permanent feature on his face. "Trust me, Newhart."

"I hate it when you talk in riddles."

"How's the leg?"

Newhart frowned. "Better. You're mighty strange, Mason. Did I ever tell you that?"

Mason patted his friend's arm. "Many times, but not as strange as the world in which we find ourselves. Now, you sit nice and easy and keep following."

Newhart shook his head, waited for Mason to set off on the trail again, and flicked the reins across the nag's back. The wagon creaked and groaned and before long, the journey recommenced. But Newhart, disturbed by Mason's curious conversation, took to glancing out across the scrub and the occasional hill several times. Perhaps Indians caused Mason to be so peculiar, so he sat up straighter and allowed his hand to rest on the revolver in his waistband. If trouble was ahead, he wanted to be ready.

* * *

The night came creeping in. For the first time in weeks, possibly months, a few wisps of cloud floated lazily across the sky and Skinner found himself counting them.

One of the other riders edged up alongside. "You think it might storm?"

Skinner shook his head and licked his lips. "We'll attack them tonight, whilst they sleep. Then we take their bodies down to Bovey, claim the reward. We should be back with Hamblin in two days, no more."

"Bovey? I thought the plan was to head on over to Salt Lake?"

Skinner shrugged. "That's a journey of weeks." He waved his hand towards the sky. "We'll get caught in a mess of weather if we delay. Best try our luck at Bovey. From what I hear, they still have a sheriff there. And a bank."

"You think those two will make a fight of it?"

"No doubt, but they won't stand a chance. We go in hard and we don't stop shooting until they're dead. They won't have an inkling of what's about to occur, so we should be fine."

"Some of the men, they're kind of nervous about all this, Skinner. They're questioning the righteousness of it. I mean, *killing*. It isn't right."

Skinner eased himself around in his saddle. "Nolan, you're a good man, as are the others, but sometimes we have to do things which otherwise might appear unsavory, unjustifiable even. But those two," he shook his head, "they are killers, rapists, bank robbers. The worst kind of humanity, Nolan, sent by the devil to bring misery and death to all they encounter. We will be ridding this land of their scourge. I've prayed hard on this, Nolan, don't think I haven't, and I am convinced, nay, *assured* that Our Heavenly Father's hand is in this. What we are doing is a good thing, the *right* thing. Cast aside your doubts, and those of the men too. In a few short hours, it will all be over and our duty will be done. Amen."

Nolan nodded. "Amen."

"Now, go tell the others to load up their weapons and prepare to ride into the camp. I'll scout ahead, check those two villains are asleep, then we attack."

Nolan turned away to do as he was bid and Skinner closed his eyes and repeated the same prayer for strength and courage he had said to himself since he left Hamblin's camp.

* * *

Skinner edged forward wormlike on his stomach, wriggling towards the ridge which overlooked the camp Newhart and Mason had set up. The wagon stood silent, the nag and Mason's horse a little way off. From this angle, he could clearly see the two men huddled up, illuminated by the campfire and the moon, flat out asleep. He smiled to himself, rolled over in a sitting position and scrambled back to where Nolan and the rest waited.

"All righty, they're asleep. Nolan, you Devon and James, you swing around from the left, Miles and Arthur, you come with me. We hit them from both sides, and we start shooting as soon as we hit the camp, you understand?" The men all grunted. "We circle around the fire and we keep putting bullets into them until we have none left. That Mason, he seems to have some sort of invisible shield around him. Well, I mean to blast it into oblivion and him along with it. As soon as we're done, we get them into the wagon and come morning, we take them to Bovey." He pulled out his revolver and checked it. "Now, before we get to it, let us pray."

* * *

The plan worked precisely as Skinner meant it too. The two groups came out of the night at a gallop, focusing in on the small campfire. The nag and Mason's horse screamed, bucked and reared up, giving the two killers a moment's warning, but not enough to cause them to spring up and defend themselves. Caught unawares, they had no time to respond. Skinner's men wheeled around in a sort of caracole, guns blazing, bullets smacking into the bodies, Skinner concentrating on the larger of the two, knowing this was Mason. He was not prepared to take any chances, so he reined in his horse, which reared up like the mount of an avenging angel, and he emptied his revolver into the body. Without a pause, he pulled out his second gun and repeated the action until the hammer clicked on empty cylinders.

The others did the same, emptying their guns, pouring bullets into the bodies.

Within less than two minutes, with the cordite lingering thick above the inert shapes, and the sound of the gunfire ringing out across the plains, the grim episode ended and silence settled.

The men, breathing hard, stared down from the saddles of their terrified horses, whose eyes glared white in the darkness. No one spoke, all of them gaping at the results of their deeds, the realization of what they had done slowly striking home. One or two sobbed, others put their faces in their hands. Only Skinner remained motionless. He holstered his gun and slipped down from his horse. He stepped around the fire and prodded Mason with his boot.

"What the hell?" was all he managed to say.

From out of the wagon they came, Newhart and Mason, clad in their underwear, guns in fists and Mason was laughing, the wild, insane cackling of a mad beast. His gun belched fire, choosing his targets whilst Newhart blazed away uncontrollably beside him. The heavy booms from their large-caliber handguns filled the night air with the frightening sound of death. The men fell, chests and heads blown apart and Skinner, speechless, staring in disbelief as he witnessed his companions fall and die all around him.

When it was over, Mason walked forward through the smoke, teeth clenched, gun aimed directly towards Skinner, who moaned, mouth dribbling, tears rolling down his face. He dropped to his knees, hands clasped in front of him. "Oh merciful Father, please. Forgive me. It wasn't me, I swear, it was Hamblin, Hamblin's plan. Please, oh sweet God, please."

Mason shook his head and spat onto the ground. "You fucking Bible-bashers, you always plead to God for what you want, whether it be the deaths of your enemies or the saving of your own pathetic skins. Well, God ain't listening brother, but I sure as hell is." He put the muzzle of his Navy Colt revolver against Skinner's head and squeezed the trigger.

A loud, dull clunk followed. The gun was empty.

"Ah shit," said Mason.

"Thank God," said Skinner and he went to stand.

Without pause, Mason, anger overcoming him, reached to the rear of his belt and brought out the broad bladed knife he kept there, and slipped it deep into Skinner's guts. The man groaned and Mason jerked the knife arm upwards, slicing open Skinner's torso to the breastbone.

Skinner went into spasm, the blood and entrails frothing out into the night air. His body went slack, slid from the blade and hit the ground with a hollow thud.

Mason watched the man squirm and die then looked over to Newhart, who was busily reloading his handguns. "You wanna burn these bastards now, or wait until tomorrow?"

"I'm tired," said Newhart, "let's leave it 'til tomorrow. Besides, the buzzards can have 'em."

"Yeah. 'Bout time we gave something back."

They both laughed then went back into the wagon, stretched themselves out and fell into thankful sleep.

Twenty-three

On the morning Simms and the others set off north to the ranch, where the lawman hoped to find Elisabeth Russell, Lieutenant Calhoon rode out at the head of a troop of twenty-four men, riding on mules. They made their way across country, by-passing the ruined homestead that Simms had found some days before, and farther on, paid scant attention to the graves of the soldiers whom Simms had buried. They camped out on the prairie, with the stars their only light, shivering beneath their blankets for Calhoon ordered no fires to be lit. Outriders, ranging ahead, had returned with news. There was a large party of men and wagons inching their way towards the Colorado River. Calhoon, chomping on a cigar, huddled around a map stretched out in the dirt. He bobbed his head.

"I reckon it's them. A detachment of Saints, making their way towards Ives. We have to prevent their advance, turn them back."

"And kill them?" asked a sour-faced sergeant, face grizzled, lined with the experience of former battles.

"As many as we can."

"Not sure the boys are up to that, Lieutenant," put in the sergeant without daring to catch Calhoon's eyes.

"I couldn't give a good fuck what they are *up to*, Sergeant. They will follow orders."

"Yes sir," said the sergeant, coming to attention.

"Shouldn't be long," said Calhoon and folded up the map. He returned the sergeant's salute, then retired to his tent where he spent most of the night partaking from one of the three bottles of whiskey he'd secreted in his saddle bags.

* * *

Unaware of the events which were developing in the other directions, Simms and his two companions rode across the rolling, broken landscape in silence. Occasionally Simms would stop, strike a match to check the map with a compass, get his bearings from the position of the sun, and continue. After the third time he did this, Winterton pushed his mule alongside the Pinkerton.

"How do you know all this stuff?" he asked.

Simms, whose horse edged away from the mule, wary of its size and strangeness, shrugged. "I told you, I was in the regular army for many years. You don't lead a troop without knowing which way to go."

"You fought Mexicans, so they say in camp."

"Mexicans, Comanche, sometimes even Apaches, but I never had much quarrel with those people. The Mexicans were the real enemy, but we scourged the land, made it into a dreadful, unforgiving place, and we killed far too many innocents. It's not something I like to talk about. Other than what I've already said."

Winterton twisted his mouth, considering Simms's words. "Seems to me suffering is something you wear like a second skin, mister."

"Who can say?"

The soldier nodded and allowed his mule to drop behind. Simms twisted in his saddle and saw him join Ableman. They were good men and Simms had to admit he had developed a grudging respect for them both. Ordinary men, torn from their families and homes, marched out here to this bleak, barren land, to face… what? Deprivation, fear, death? He suspected all they ever really thought about was their homes, their loved ones left behind, with precious little opportunity to communicate. He himself experienced the same, the endless weeks, months sometimes, without a word. He remembered the look on his mother's face when he finally arrived home. She crumpled in his arms, sobbing like a baby whilst Father stood on the porch steps, looking like a man whose every prayer had been answered. When Simms applied for the Pinkertons, Mother took to her bed. She never got out of it. Within six months, both of his parents were dead. Now, there was no one to write home to or receive letters from. Perhaps it was better that way. He sighed, turned to face north again and let his chin drop to his chest, trying his best to sleep.

* * *

As the dawn spread clear across the horizon, scouts returned with news of the Mormon's progress and Calhoon ordered his men to dismount and spread out in a long line. Whilst three soldiers remained behind to tend to the mules, the rest set off across the scrubland, rifles at the ready.

But if Calhoon was hoping to take the Mormon party unawares, he was wrong. Their own out-riders had informed their leader, and they knelt behind whatever cover they could find and set off a steady stream of fire as the soldiers emerged.

"Kneel boys," shouted Calhoon, brandishing his Navy Colt. Bullets filled the air, hissing overhead, cutting through the thick air in red-hot trails. The soldiers responded with almost clockwork precision, the sergeant ordering them to, "Aim and prepare to fire." He swatted the air with his revolver and the first volley erupted across the plain like the roar of a gigantic beast from a mythical past.

As the soldiers feverishly reloaded, Calhoon paraded along their length. They were in the open, with no cover, which perturbed Calhoon not at all. He squinted across the space that separated his troops from the Mormon militia, saw bullets pinging off rocks, and felt confident his men would endure.

The second volley roared, twenty rifled muskets sending their pieces of lead towards the enemy with no more success than if they were launching snowballs in the sunshine. Calhoon swore and beckoned the sergeant to draw closer.

"From this range our fire is ineffective, so we need to outflank them. Send a group of six men over yonder," he indicated a rolling patch of prairie covered with gorse and brush, "and set up an enfilading fire on their position. In the meantime, we shall advance."

"Towards them, sir?"

"What part of the word 'advance' do you not understand, sergeant?"

"But some of the boys will get hit, Lieutenant. They might die."

"That's their job, sergeant. So let's crack to it."

Yet again, Calhoon's plan fizzled out into failure. No sooner had his sergeant moved off towards the gorse, than some of the Mormons broke cover and raced forward themselves, firing their handguns from the hip. One or two of Calhoon's troop wavered and took up a fearful yelling, fear causing hands to fumble, ramrods to clatter to the ground, precious cartridges spilling. Calhoon spat into the dust and strode forward, levelled his Navy Colt and shot one of the Mormon's in the head.

The others turned and fled.

Calhoon sighed and holstered his gun as the remaining enemy militia became like ghosts on the prairie. He watched them scrambling around, squawking and screaming amongst themselves, battling with wagons and horses, panic racing through each and every one.

"Damn it all to hell," spat Calhoon, noting his sergeant trudging mournfully towards him.

"Orders, sir?"

"Forget it," said Calhoon. "This whole goddamned adventure was doomed to failure before it even started."

"But you got one of them at least."

"You think so? Take a look."

And the sergeant did, staring in disbelief as the man Calhoon 'shot' got to his knees, stuck a forefinger through a hole in his hat, and raised his face skywards to give praise to his god. Then he turned and ran like a jack-rabbit, back to his companions. Together, they retreated into the distance in a mass of swirling dust and general mayhem.

"Dear God," breathed the sergeant.

Calhoon put a cigar between his teeth. "Blessed, that's what they are, sergeant – blessed." He watched the quickly diminishing militia for a long time before he said, "We head for the river, tell Ives what we intend to do. I doubt there'll be much trouble now, at least not until the spring."

"That's a long time. Lieutenant. Will we be spending Thanksgiving on the Colorado?"

Calhoon arched an eyebrow. "Christmas, too."

The sergeant's crestfallen expression gave Calhoon a clear indication of the delights waiting for them all over the next few months.

* * *

Simms held up his hand and waited for the others to roll up and join him.

Ableman was breathing with some difficulty and he appeared sullen, skin waxy, eyes lackluster. Simms studied him but said nothing. "That must be it," he said.

Sitting alone, the towering hills as a backdrop, the ranch gleamed resplendent and new looking. From this distance, it appeared little more than a toy so Simms pulled out the telescope and focused in on it.

The front door was closed, nobody stirred. Away to the right, fenced fields, with a scattering of cattle in one, horses in another. He wondered about that and lowered the eyepiece. "Strange to have horses out in the open like that, with Indians so close. Makes me think…" He shifted his weight in the saddle. "Well, whatever, we have to go and investigate. Keep your hands well away from your guns. These aren't desperadoes, my friends. These are good people."

"How can you be sure?"

"Because Elisabeth Randall wouldn't stay with them if they weren't."

"And how do you know she's there?"

"I don't, but I have a feeling. Ableman, are you feeling up to this?"

The big man managed to raise his head. He let out a low moan.

Winterton reached across and touched Ableman's face. He immediately pulled his hand back. "He's cold and clammy. What the hell's the matter with him?"

"Sunstroke or dehydration, maybe both." Simms unstopped his canteen and thrust it towards Ableman's mouth. "Drink."

Ableman turned away, moaning again.

"Let's go," said Simms, putting the canteen away. "But keep alert. I don't think these people are dangerous, but they may be scared, overly-nervous and that may make them trigger-happy. Keep your wits about you."

Winterton nodded and spurred his mule, which reluctantly plodded forward.

The closer they came, the more Simms took in of the house, marveling at its pristine condition, the broad veranda with the rocking chairs laid out neatly upon it, more of a hotel than a dwelling. He kept glancing across to the fenced fields, the barn and other outhouses. He thought he caught a movement there, but without stopping to take a closer look, he couldn't be sure. So he continued on, his horse kicking up the dust.

At about twenty or so paces from the house, the front door eased open and a young man appeared, black trousers held up by braces, black, high-crowned hat on his heads, twin-barreled shotgun in his arms.

Simms stopped, the two behind following suit.

Everyone waited.

From around the corner of the house appeared another man, rifle in hands, and again, on the opposite corner, another. From the central dormer window, a woman, squinting along the barrel of an ancient-looking musket. No one spoke.

Simms, as slowly as possible, raised both hands, and drawled out the corner of his mouth, "Do the same, boys. Show them we mean no harm."

The move did not result in a response, not at first. The man in the doorway stepped forward, his boots sounding loud on the wooden slats. He tilted his head.

"We have nothing for you here, friend," said the man.

"I think maybe you have."

The man frowned and swung the shotgun around, in the proximity of Simms's gut. He eased back both hammers. "I think maybe not. You have precisely five seconds to turn around and get off our land." He nodded towards Winterton and Ableman. "Federal men or not, this is private property."

"My name is Simms."

"That's *one*."

"And I'm here on official business..."

"Two."

"I mean no harm and I do not wish to—"

"Three."

"Jesus, Simms," hissed Winterton.

"I'm a Pinkerton detective."

"Four. We're opening up on you at five."

"And I'm looking for Elisabeth Randall."

The man on the veranda froze, his body rocking backwards slightly. His grip weakened on the shotgun and slowly it lowered. "Who?"

Simms nodded, "Elisabeth Randall, daughter of General Randall, kidnapped by two desperadoes. Killers. I believe she may be here, or at least has passed this way, and if she has I have some important news for her and would ask you to point me in the direction she took."

"News?" asked a voice, and from within the house stepped a young woman. Strikingly good looking, hair tied back in a bun, dressed in a plain white pinafore over a long, trailing dress. "What kind of news?"

Simms slowly lowered his hands. "Elisabeth Randall?"

"What news?"

"Your father. He's alive."

Twenty-four

At the dining table, with the main meal of stew, dumplings and sweet potatoes coming to an end, Winterton sat back in his chair, beaming, and patted his stomach with both hands. "I have to say, that is the finest meal I've had since my dear mama still lived!"

They all smiled, some laughed. Across the table, Simms carefully put down his knife and fork over his empty plate and dabbed at his mouth with a serviette. "I concur, Miss Randall. That really was quite delicious."

At the end of the table, beside the young man who stood in the doorway with a shotgun, Elisabeth blushed a little, her head down. "Well, thank you, but really, it was nothing special. Just a pot of rib steak and beans."

"A feast," piped up another, older man who sat at the far end. "As always."

Lots of nodding and muttering of agreement followed.

"I have to say," continued Simms, putting down his serviette, "given the deprivations of this land, it is a miracle you have managed to sustain yourself to such a degree."

"Our Heavenly Father provides the miracle, friend," said the man next to Elisabeth.

"And we provide the muscle to till the good earth," said the other young man sitting adjacent to him.

Simms nodded. "Yes, yes I see that, but even so… the land is ravaged. It hasn't rained since I don't remember when. The natives are restless, many of them moving farther west to escape, to find better land. Many of them are dying in the process."

"We are friendly with the natives," put in Elisabeth. "Many pass this way and we welcome them into our home. We have no arguments with them and once they have sat at our table, and been blessed by Our Heavenly Father, they leave as friends."

"Well, whatever it is you're doing, it is working," said Simms, smiling down at his plate. "We're mighty grateful."

"We sure are," said Winterton. He glanced across at Ableman who remained sullen, chin on chest, a film of grease and gravy around his mouth. "Are you all right, Chuck?"

Ableman did not respond.

Elisabeth stood and took to tidying away the remnants of the meal, stacking empty plates on top of one another, whilst the other women bustled about, clearing away other bits and pieces.

"He needs rest," said the man at the head of the table, "a bath, clean clothes."

"We all do," said Winterton, but the look of concern ran deep in his features. "But, he must have some sort of fever. The detective here said it might be sunstroke."

"I thought it was, now I'm not so sure."

"Well," said the man, "I think it best if we put him to bed, keep him quiet. Jacob, will you prepare a good, hot bath for our guest?"

Jacob, the second young man, nodded his head, pushed back his chair and disappeared into the depths of the house.

Simms propped his elbows on the table. "The men who came. Can you tell me about them?"

For a moment the most awful stillness settled over the two remaining men. They exchanged a look before the man at the head of the table sighed. "They came in a covered wagon, with Elisabeth. I could tell, right from the very moment they came into sight, that something was not quite right. Father saw them first, told us to take up our guns.

He had never said such a thing before, not once since we were led to this place by the good Lord."

"And what happened?"

The man's eyes closed briefly. "We did not know it, but the larger of the two, the one we came to know as Mason, circled around back. When the shooting started, he broke in like the demon he is, and although we fired shot after shot, none hit him."

"A devil, Job, that's what he was," said the other.

"No," said Job. "Peter, all of us have prayed hard on this. I know you find such things difficult to understand, not being of our faith, but the man is no devil. He is a human being just like any other, but changed, warped if you like."

"Either way," said Peter, his voice low, dangerous, "what he did…"

"And he got away?" interjected Simms.

Job steepled his fingers, his jaw line tightening. "Yes, but not before he killed my father and our maid. Later on, Elisabeth told us of her suffering at the hand of this man. We could not believe anyone could treat another with such bestiality."

"You'd be surprised what you can find out in the world," said Simms with meaning. "It is my desire to hunt him down and bring him to justice. For what he did to Miss Randall, for what he continues to do to others."

"Well, you're a lawman," said Peter, "it must come easy. I have lain awake at night, thinking of it, thinking I could go after them, but—"

"Can you tell me in which direction he headed?"

Job shrugged his shoulders, "North-west. Elisabeth told us he often talked about going up to the Colorado. Apparently there is a ferry there. He and his partner often talked about re-supplying themselves from there, although only God knows how they planned on doing that."

"By killing," said Simms. "Those two men, Newhart and Mason, they will stop at nothing to take what they want."

"But you have their measure, detective."

"That I do. If Mason will not come peacefully, then I shall kill him, without hesitation."

"Thou shall not kill," murmured Job.

"Sir, I have killed more than I can remember, out on this prairie and in the War between this country and the Mexicans. It is not something which bothers me much nowadays, I have to say."

"Were all those you killed deserving of dying, Mr. Simms?"

"I would say so. The first man I killed was a member of a bunch of Mexican raiders on the border, pillaging a smallholding, having murdered the men folk. They were turning their attention to the women when my troop came upon them. I shot that bastard right between the eyes and didn't think nothing of it." He paused, mind going back to that moment. "We didn't take any prisoners."

The others looked at him, including Winterton, who stared but didn't speak.

"I've lost count of those I've killed and seen killed," continued Simms, "and I have not one regret for anything I have done. The suffering those men visited upon others condemned them, in my eyes. To use your parlance, I was a servant of Lord God Almighty in ridding the land of such scum."

"The Lord *God Almighty* does not sanctify the killing of fellow human beings."

"He may not, not directly, but He sure as hell did not do anything to stop me."

Leaning forward, Job's voice dropped in tone, serious and intense, "Detective, we are God-fearing folk here. We defended ourselves, as best we could but we do not revel in the killing of others, even those whom we find to be intolerant, bestial even. It is Our Heavenly Father who will judge."

"And yet your people gather arms against the Federal government. You muster your militia and make ready to defend yourselves. Is that not an acceptance of killing for a just cause?"

Job sat back, his face reddening whilst Peter, head lowered, remained in silence for a long time. Clearing his throat, Job eventually said, "I cannot speak for those over in Salt Lake, Mr. Simms. All I know is, our earthly father was a man of peace. He taught us to accept others, to welcome them, treat them with kindness. Those are the principles we use with the native Indians, and it has proved sound council in our dealings with them."

"But not with Mason."

The man's eyes clouded over and he lowered his gaze. "No. Not with Mason."

"The man is an abomination," interjected Peter and was about to say more when the women returned. He sat back and folded his arms.

Elisabeth smiled and sat down beside Simms. "How long before we leave?"

The stunned silence, which followed, was matched by Simms's wide-eyed surprise. "I didn't think you—"

"I wish to visit my father," she said, bright and cheerful. "I have discussed it with Ann and Sarah. Once I have seen him, I shall return here to live, as I have chosen to do." She leaned forward, her eyes cold, lending weight to her words, "This is my home now, Detective."

"A might dangerous one, if I say so," said Winterton.

"Well, I'm sure Detective Simms will set that all aright," she said and gave Simms a lingering look, "won't you, Detective?"

"I will."

"Well, there we are." She sat back, beaming. "I presume we shall return to Fort Bridger, where I will wait for you. When you return, we shall travel east to where father is staying."

"That's a fair way. But..." Simms could not help but smile, "You seem to have it all planned, Miss Randall."

"Oh, I do. I am eager to see him once again, Detective. I thought I had lost him. You can't begin to understand what it feels like; to know he is still alive."

"I think I can."

"Have you any family, Detective?" asked Sarah.

"No. I'm not sure I could do what I do, if I had."

Sarah nodded, almost as if she knew the truth of what Simms said. Perhaps she did.

"And you have no one else," asked Elisabeth, "no sweetheart?"

Simms ran a finger under his collar as the heat rose to his cheeks. "I, er, wouldn't go so far as to say that, Miss Randall, no."

"Ah," Elisabeth smiled, looking around the table to each of her 'family' in turn, "I guess from the sound of your voice that there may well be someone?"

Simms squirmed in his chair, his discomfort clear for all to see. Winterton laughed and Simms shot him a hard stare.

"There may be. I have to say it was not something I was looking for, but..." He shrugged, uncomfortable at being the center of attention.

"Ah," Elisabeth's smile broadened, "I knew it! Detective Simms, I do not believe you are as hard as you make out. Who is she?"

"No one," said Simms quickly and stood up, "I'd best go and check the horses."

"They're all watered and fed," said Peter, "have no fear."

"Even so." Simms forced a smile towards Elisabeth. "Thank you again for the supper."

And Elisabeth rocked back in her chair, continuing to smile as Simms left.

Twenty-five

The town's main street was broad, lined with offices and stores, together with a smattering of hotels, saloons and various other eating-places. Side streets branched off in all directions and set back a little, on a small premonitory, was a sizeable church, its tower plainly seen from where Newhart and Mason sat, taking it all in.

"What do you think?" asked Newhart, sagging with the heat.

"I don't know," said Mason cautiously, scanning the many buildings for any signs of life. There didn't appear to be much. Tied up at the occasional hitching rail, a tired-looking mule or bedraggled horse, farther down, broken carts and wagons, a stack of shattered crates, and deep ruts in the roadway proclaiming the coming and going of many horse drawn vehicles. The entire town stood silent and depressed, almost as if the residents of this forlorn place had left in a great hurry.

"I'm going to the saloon," said Mason, pointing to the closest building across the street. "You tie up the horses and wagon, but stay with them. God alone knows what sorts of varmints are lurking behind the shutters. If you get a chance, have a look for a livery stable. I need the horse re-shod."

Newhart grunted and Mason got down from his horse, adjusted his belt and hat and shuffled across the street.

He pushed open the double swing doors and stepped inside.

The room was dark, tables arranged haphazardly across the floor, all covered with dust. To the right, a long bar and behind it a fine-looking mirror, engraved with the words 'Harwell and Jackson, Gold Mine Inc' set in a semi-circle across the top. The writing may once have been in gold, now it was faded and chipped.

Mason allowed his eyes to roam over the room. Directly ahead was a back door, and to his left, a steep staircase which led to a balcony. From where he stood, he could just see the tops of further rooms. He rolled his shoulders and went over to the counter.

Learning across, he saw a neat array of empty bottles, filthy with grime, but above them, on the shelf, were several half-full with amber liquid. Mason licked his lips. He couldn't remember the last time he'd tasted good whisky.

"A dollar a glass," came a voice.

Mason stood rigid as he studied the reflection of a small, bald-headed man in the mirror. He carried a shotgun, which he levelled directly towards Mason. "That's mighty steep," Mason breathed through clenched teeth.

"And business is mighty slow. Now, ease your hands flat on the countertop, stranger, and don't make no sudden movements."

"Wouldn't dream of it," said Mason and did as he was told.

The man moved slowly to the far end of the bar, pulled open a hinged door and stepped through the gap to the other side. With the gun trained unerringly towards Mason, he made his way along until he stood opposite. "If you're looking for anything to eat, we ain't got any."

Mason nodded, eyes settling on the twin barrels of the gun. "Would you mind putting that away, or at least pointing it somewhere else? It's making me nervous."

"I couldn't give a goddamned fuck what it makes you. What do you want here?"

Mason gave a short laugh. "Well, nothing you got, that's for sure. Is there anywhere that has food, water, a bed for the night?"

"Maybe Casey's, way down the end of the street. I believe he still takes guests, although I do believe he'll be packing away as soon as he is able."

"Why the rush to leave?"

"Ain't nothing here. Hasn't been for years, not since the gold rush petered out. Then the miners took to hiring themselves out as gun hands, to butcher Indians. Is you a miner?"

"Do I look like one?"

"You look like nobody I've ever seen. A regulator maybe? I hear them Mormons are hiring killers to assassinate army officers out on the trail."

"Well, I'm not one of them either. I'm just passing through, trying to make my way west, find a piece of land. Nothing more."

"You with other people?" Mason nodded. "Where's the rest of you?"

"Family is way yonder," he indicated the street beyond the swing doors. "We've had it mighty bad these past days, what with Indians and the lack of water."

"Bull," hissed the man. "I saw you coming down the street, watched you. You ain't got no family. Who is the other guy?"

"A friend." Mason frowned. "My wife and child are in the wagon. Mister, why are you so suspicious, and if I may say, so damned unfriendly?"

"Because I know your kind, mister. You wear them guns like a gunfighter. And your eyes tell me you're a killer."

"Is that so?"

"Yes it is."

"I'd still like a whisky. Maybe some milk for my child."

Mason grinned and the man frowned, some of his suspicions slipping away. The shotgun lowered slightly. It was enough.

In a blur of movement, Mason's hands streaked out to snatch away the gun from his interrogator's relaxed grip, yanked it free and slammed the stock full into the man's face, sending him crashing back amongst the bottles and glasses. He slumped to the floor, face shattered, blood spilling down across his shirtfront. He moaned then slid to his left and remained still.

Mason checked the shotgun before settling it down on the counter top. He vaulted over, kicking away the glass, and found one of the half-empty bottles. He pulled out the stopper and raised it to his lips.

"What the hell?"

The swinging doors creaked and a man stood there, silhouetted against the daylight. Mason, with the bottle still to his lips, drew his revolver with his other hand and shot the man through the chest, the force of the gunshot sending him sprawling out in the street.

Outside somebody started screaming, but Mason ignored it, taking another huge mouthful from the bottle.

"My, that tastes good."

Another man burst in through the door, bent low, fanning his six-shooter, bullets whistling through the room in a wild spray. Mason hunched up his shoulders and crouched down below the counter, waiting for the blasting to cease. When it did, he rose up, saw the second man hastily reloading his gun, took careful aim, and shot him in the head. The man pitched backwards to the ground, eyes wide open, blood blossoming around him on the floor.

Mason holstered his gun, and taking the shotgun under the crook of his arm, strolled around the counter and went into the daylight.

In the street was a horse-drawn wagon. On her knees, beside the first man Mason shot, was a woman dressed in a dark blue dress, tight jacket over the top and tied bonnet on her head. She was wailing, cradling the dead man's head in her lap. Mason took a drink and clumped down the steps. He set off across the street to where Newhart had tied up their wagon.

He found Newhart in the reception area of a deserted hotel, sat in a rocking chair, head lolling, fast asleep. He went over and kicked his feet. Newhart sat up, eyes darting around. "Mason? What the hell is going on?"

"Nothing." He looked around him. "This place has to be the weirdest I've ever come across. It's as if someone just came along and plucked every single person from off of their feet and spirited them away."

"It's a ghost town. It must have been a grand place once."

"Yeah, well..." Mason handed the bottle over to Newhart, who looked upon it as if it were the most wonderful treasure he had ever seen. With great reverence, he pulled out the stopper, breathed in the aroma and closed his eyes in obvious ecstasy. Then he drank.

The woman came in. She was like something possessed, face tear stained, hair disheveled, teeth gnashing. In her hand was a revolver. Mason quickly crossed the room, twisted her wrist. She squealed and the gun fell from her fingers. He back-handed her across the face. She crumpled and he caught her around the waist.

"Who the hell is she?"

Mason looked at his friend and shrugged. "I don't rightly know but I guess she's kinda upset. I think it was her husband I shot."

"Oh hell, Mason, why do you have to go 'round killing everyone?"

"I don't," he said, and winked. He lifted up the woman in his arms and moved easily towards a row of doorways at the far end of the room. "I do other things, too."

* * *

Later, in the cool of the evening, Newhart sat out on the porch, his feet crossed on the hitching rail, staring into nothing. He rested a large tumbler of whisky on his stomach. His jacket was on the back of his rocking chair, his hat next to it. As far as he could recall, this was the first time in months he had sat and rested. He sighed, closed his eyes, and let his thoughts wander.

A footfall roused him and he opened one eye to see Mason stepping up to the rail. He was bare-chested, hat on his head, a cigar in his mouth. He puffed at it, put both hands on the rail and let out a long breath. "She was a wild cat," he said and blew out a long stream of smoke."

"You left her in the room? Jesus, Mason, she could—"

Mason shook his head and grunted, holding up his right hand, the cigar between the first two fingers. "No, no, don't fret none, Newhart. The girl, she's sleeping."

"Contented?"

Mason shrugged. "Like I say, this is a weird place. She didn't want nothing to do with me. I can't fathom it. You know," he took a pull of the cigar, "I'm a-thinking this might be a fine place to rest up a little whiles, relax, take stock of the situation. For all we know, there might be some rich pickings hereabouts."

"I doubt it."

"Well, tomorrow I propose we take a good look around, see what there is remaining in this here wonderful town of Bovey."

"Is that its name?"

"So my lady friend tells me, when she decided to talk. Seems it all collapsed after the goldmines petered out. It took some time before folk realized the enormity of that, and then they started moving away. They held on, so she says, but nothing changed. She said it was always her husband's plan to come here, and then to move."

"She ain't sore at you, for killing him?"

"Well…" He pushed himself away from the rail, straightening out his arms, "she was at first, but after a short while, with the help of some whisky, she opened up, got to realizing life with me might be a whole lot more preferable to being with her husband. She'd taken to sharing his brother's bed, but she found him as wanting in the romance department as her beloved."

"Don't suppose she can say the same about you?"

"No sir-ee. When I convince her of my charms, she won't want it to stop, Newhart. When it comes to loving, I am what you might call an expert."

Newhart swallowed. "Damn, wish I could find me a girl."

"Well, you might. Like I say, we'll take a scout around at first light. Did you say you found some food?"

"There's some beans and peas in the back room. Not much, but I reckon I could rustle up a stew of sorts."

"Well, you do just that my friend. I shall go and visit my good lady again, see if I can convince her to open them soft thighs of hers!"

Newhart watched him go and cursed softly. "Goddamn you, Mason, when am I going to partake of the fruits of the tree?"

But Mason didn't hear. He strolled back to his room and pushed open the door, half expecting to find his prospective lover stretched out naked on the bed, begging him to show her affection. But she wasn't. Instead, she was behind the door and he never felt the blow, which cracked down on his skull, so hard it sent the world spinning out of all recognition.

Out on the porch, Newhart rocked back a few times on his chair, then stood up. A stew would suit, although he would have preferred some meat, perhaps a little bread. At least they could wash it down with some good whisky.

He turned around and felt his stomach turn over. He gaped. The woman, wearing nothing but a thin shift, had the barrel of Mason's Navy Colt pointing straight at him. She held it in two hands and it seemed terribly big. Her eyes were fixed, determined, not to be argued with.

"Don't go for your gun, mister. I'm a dead-eye shot."

Newhart nodded, "Now, if that be the truth, I would ask you not to be thinking to shoot me, ma'am."

"Take out your gun, throw it away, then drop the gun belt or I'll blow you in half." And she eased back the hammer.

"Please," he cried, "I'll do it." And he did, deftly picking his revolver out of the holster with forefinger and thumb. He threw it down, where it fell with a dull thud on the wooden slats of the boardwalk. The belt followed. He watched her come forward, and kick the gun away out of reach.

"I'm taking your wagon," she said. "If you come after me, I'll not go out without a fight. You bastards, what you did to me, killing my man…" She sobbed, tears sprouting.

"Mason told me your husband was a—"

"You keep your filthy trap shut about my husband, you son of a bitch. That *Mason*, he's a rutting bull, thinking he's God's gift. Well, he ain't. He's a stinking piece of filth. I'd rather see him dead than spend another second with him." She motioned with the Colt. "Get out of the way."

"Have you killed him?"

"No, but I will kill you if you do not move."

Newhart did so, stepping aside, his arms now raised high above his head. "We'll come after you," he said.

"And I'll be waiting, like I said. And I'll kill you, like the filthy beasts you are."

Keeping the gun trained on him, she slowly descended the steps from the porch onto the dirt. She looked around and then set off towards the nag at a run.

Newhart watched her for a moment, then crossed the room at a run towards the back room where he found Mason, groaning, the back of his head thick with black blood. He got down and rolled his friend onto his back.

"Well, this is a fine pickle."

Mason's eyes fluttered open. He grinned. "I told you she was a wildcat."

Twenty-six

There was a good deal of hugging and kissing before Elisabeth, Simms and the others set off once more, this time towards Fort Bridger and the Federal camp.

At one point, as they were about to ride over the far side of the escarpment, she looked back to see the white-fronted ranch house standing bright and clean in the distance. She thought she saw them all, standing on the veranda, waving, but she couldn't be sure.

"They're good people," said Simms.

"Yes," she said, and brushed away the tear, which rolled down her cheek. "They took me in without question, never judging me. I will return to them as soon as I have talked to my father."

"I'll ask Colonel Johnston to send a telegram, see if we can arrange a meeting. It may mean you taking a train back east."

"I know. How long, do you think, before I return? Three months?"

"Maybe. Might be more. Depends how this so-called war develops."

She nodded, sniffed loudly and turned her horse away. Simms soon settled in behind her.

They buried Ableman on the morning of the second day. They found him laid out as if asleep, under his blanket, head propped up on his saddle. Winterton discovered his demise when he failed to rouse him and he knelt down beside his friend and remained there for a long time, in silence.

At Fort Bridger, late that same day, Winterton took the horses and his mule to be fed and watered, whilst Simms escorted Elisabeth to Colonel Johnston's command tent.

"I didn't think you'd make it," the Colonel said, standing up from behind his desk. He came around and shook Elisabeth's hand. "I'm glad you did. I knew your father. A great soldier and a considerate man." He looked across to Simms. "You'll be completing your duty; I suppose?"

"I have some leads. I will return to the ferry, speak to Calhoon and Ives. My quarry was said to be moving that way. If either have seen them, then I might gain some vital information as to the direction they took."

"Well, I wish you well, Detective." He smiled across to Elisabeth. "It might be for the best if you stayed here, in my quarters. I shall organize whatever you need. I shall take over Calhoon's tent, so all will be well. No doubt you will be anxious to leave to meet your father, so I shall send telegrams, see what can be ascertained."

Elisabeth smiled. "Thank you."

"I would be grateful if you could send my headquarters a word or two about my situation," said Simms. Johnston nodded.

"And thank you, Detective," said Elisabeth, turning on her heels. She reached up and planted a kiss on his cheek. "You take care out there. That man is a monster."

"I know it." Simms brought himself to attention and saluted Johnston, who returned it, and then he left without another word.

* * *

Simms made his farewells to Winterton later that same day, deciding to cut across the dry prairie at night, when it was cooler. Winterton stood and shook his hand, his sadness like a living thing, pressing down upon him. "I hate this place," he said with meaning.

"Don't we all."

"He never even got to fire his rifle."

"That might be for the best."

"I'll write a letter to his folks. We often used to talk about our home. Although I didn't know him when we lived there, I feel as if I've always been his friend. My English ain't up to much, but I believe I can convey something about what a good man he was."

"Yes. Do that. And he was brave. Anyone who rides across the plains of this Territory is brave. Mention that with feeling."

"I shall. God bless you, Detective."

"Yeah."

He rode out without another word and did not know if he would ever come back.

* * *

He met with Calhoon, Ives remaining on board the riverboat. "We had a skirmish with some Saints," said the Lieutenant. "No one died, thank God, but they fled south, I know not where."

"And no one else has come here?"

"The men you're searching for, detective, won't come within twenty miles of here if they have any sense. If the Mormons don't kill them, the Indians certainly will."

"They have a peculiar gift for staying alive."

Calhoon grunted. "Well, if they do happen to come this way, I'll not bandy with them, you have no fear on that score. I'll put them in the brig and keep 'em safe and sound until you return. That's if you don't overtake them on the range."

Simms pulled himself up into his saddle.

"You might find some advantage in talking to them Mormons. They had wagons, so they won't be moving so fast. I decided it best to remain here, otherwise I would have ridden them down myself."

Simms doffed his hat and rode out towards the direction of the Mormon troop.

* * *

In the dwindling light of the evening, he came across the pickets, and without wishing to, he spooked them. They raced to their horses, mounted and galloped off into the night, leaving him to ponder his next move.

He made a camp, without a fire, and rested until the dawn. In the morning, he shivered, pulling his blanket tight around him. He drank from his canteen and chewed on some hard tack. His back was tight, his bones frozen and he stretched out his limbs before checking his weapons and setting off towards the horizon. He did not want another night like this one for a long time.

In the basin of the prairie, he saw them and dropped to his knees to survey their gathering through the telescope.

Further to the right, he spotted the pickets and he lowered his telescope and sighed. What he did not want was for them to take his approach as threatening, so he fashioned a piece of white material from one of his shirts stuffed in his saddlebags and tied it to the end of his carbine. He mounted and set the horse to walking at a steady pace, directly towards the two waiting men, carbine held aloft with its 'flag of peace' fluttering in the slight breeze.

After words, they escorted him into the camp and a man dressed in a neat waistcoat and grey corduroy trousers stuffed into black leather boots, held court with his companions to the rear, bristling with weapons.

"You an army man?"

"Nope." Simms tilted his head and lowered the carbine. "I'm a Pinkerton."

"Well, don't that beat all," said another.

Invited into the man's tent, the guards relieved him of his guns. The man poured water and shared some with Simms. At the entrance to the tent, two big men cradled shotguns. No one spoke for a while as the water was drunk.

"I have heard it said you Pinkertons' are most honorable men."

"I like to think so," said Simms. "We discharge our duty, get the job done."

"And what is your job, sir? Siding with the Federal government to kill us, or send us to prison? Is that why you are here, to parley for Colonel Johnston before he sets his hounds upon us?"

"I heard he already has."

The man nodded. "He gave it a try, but all to no avail. We are moving back to Echo Canyon. They shall not pass."

"I'm not with the Federal government."

The man digested this news and sat down on a canvas chair. It was the only piece of furniture. He studied Simms for a moment. "Very well, if that is the case, then what is it you want from us?"

Simms nodded to the two guards, and with extreme slowness, he reached into his coat and pulled out the poster. "I have it on some authority these men are roaming the region. I wondered if you may have seen them, perhaps even come across them?"

The man leaned forward and took the poster. He grunted. Then he reached out for a heavy-looking book, bound in ruby-red leather. It creaked when he opened it. What he brought out made Simms gasp.

"These two," said the man and held up an identical poster. He looked from his own to Simms's. "We have met them, Mr. Pinkerton. We ran them off."

"Which way?"

"I believe they headed out towards Bovey. The trail runs right across the plain and through the town. It is easy to pick up, being the trail the gold-prospectors used in the Forty-Nine. But," he shifted in his chair and passed Simms' poster back to the detective, "I doubt you'll catch them alive. Not now."

Simms frowned. "I don't get your meaning."

"I have sent my men out after them. My best men. I won't lie to you, detective. It is my intention to capture those two renegades, alive or dead, and claim the reward. I would then use the money to purchase funds, to help us in our defense of Echo Canyon."

Simms took a deep breath. "I see. Your best men, you say?"

"The very best. If you decide to set off on the trail, it would be my guess you may well meet them on their way back. If you do, give them my regards. The group's commander is a man named Skinner."

"And your name, sir?"

"Ah, forgive me." The man stood up, took Simms hand and shook it briefly. "Hamblin. Jacob Hamblin, commander of the Nauvoo Legion. Perhaps on your return to Bridger, you could inform Colonel Johnston of our determination to thwart his advance. We do not wish to resort to violence, but we will do whatever is necessary to defend our way of life."

"Well, Johnston ain't figuring on campaigning until the spring. When this drought breaks, much of the landscape will become impassable. And once winter sets in..."

"Yes, quite. Let us hope by then diplomacy will have relieved the situation."

"I couldn't agree more. Killing ain't no way to solve problems... not in the long term, at least."

But killing was what he came across once more out on the trail; the bodies of Skinner and his Mormon band lying black and half-eaten by the buzzards. He saw the signs of the wagon cutting through the dirt, pulled away his neckerchief, and wiped his face with it. Then he set himself towards the direction of Bovey and did not give the dead a second thought.

Twenty-seven

His boots sounded loud on the uneven, ill-fitting floorboards and he stopped within a couple of paces, self-conscious, allowing himself a small, nervous smile. The dust, thick and grey on the floor, billowed in tiny puffs and he eased the door closed against the breeze.

A man in the corner sat at a lone table, stared, unblinking. Three others in the adjacent corner swiveled in their chairs. No one spoke. Simms revolved his shoulders a few times and took off his hat. He ran his necktie around the inside rim, put it back on and crossed to the bar.

It was a small, bright room, the sunlight from the large window on the east-facing wall casting everything in stark white. The barman polished a filthy glass with a towel which was equally grimy and his eyes were narrow against the glare.

"What can I get you, mister?"

Simms put down his portmanteau, placed his right boot on the bar rail and leaned forward. "I'd like a beer. You do have beer; I presume?"

"You presume correctly," said the barman, blowing into the glass and polishing it some more. "It's good and cold. And fifty cents."

Simms pursed his lips, but did not speak. This was the first watering-place he'd come across since leaving the camp at the Colorado River ferry some days before and he would have gladly paid a dollar, perhaps more if it meant he could slake his thirst. So he reached into the pocket of his tweed jacket and snapped a fifty-cent piece on the counter.

The barman palmed the coin away and reached for the nearby pump, and filled the glass he'd only moments before been attempting to clean, with golden, frothy beer. When finished, he slid it over. Simms stared, picked it up and blew away the first two inches or more of the froth. Smiling, he thrust it towards the barman. "Obliged if you'd fill it up."

The barman frowned. Some of the men in the corner shifted in their seats, wood creaking noisily. No one spoke and Simms continued to wait with his arm held out straight. The barman sighed, took the glass and grudgingly filled the glass up to the rim.

"Anything else?"

Simms put the glass to his lips, grunted, "Uh-huh," and drank.

The barman stared, open-mouthed as Simms's jacket fell open, revealing the Navy Colt under his left armpit, the Colt Dragoon slanting across his midriff. The man tilted his head. "You a bounty hunter?"

Someone groaned from one of the corners. Chairs scraped backwards and men stood up. Simms carefully placed the almost-finished glass on the counter and gave the men a sidelong glance. "No."

Such an admission didn't stop the men from leaving, none of them giving Simms as much as a glance. Their exit appeared a little too swift for Simms liking and he turned, leaning back against the counter, putting his thumbs into his belt. His hands were never far from his guns, the Colt Dragoon, butt out, designed for a cross-belly draw.

The door crashed shut. Only three men remained. The silent one in the other corner grunted and tilted his hat over his eyes.

"Then what the hell are you? Ain't no cowboy dresses like you, least none that I know. Jacket, good quality trousers… and two guns."

"Three," said Simms. He turned and finished his beer in one smooth movement. "But I'm not telling you where the third one is."

"On your horse?"

Simms smiled. "What's your name, friend?"

"Martinson."

"What's that, Dutch?"

"Danish, on my father's side. My mother was Swedish. Some call me Swede, others nothing at all."

Simms nodded. "You had this place long?"

"Came across here in Forty-Nine, opened it as a hardware store selling shovels and pans to the miners. When they stopped coming through, I turned it into a diner."

"A *diner*?" Simms gave the interior a roaming glance. "You mean; you actually sell food?"

"Used to. Fever took my wife last winter. Since then…" His voice trailed away. "I can fix you some bacon, cheese and bread, if you're hungry."

"That would be kind, thank you."

"Two dollars."

Simms had to laugh. "I'll have another beer, too," he said and put three coins on the counter. "Leave another in the pump until later."

He picked up his portmanteau and wandered over to the table recently abandoned by the other men. He pushed away the remnants of their drinking and their card game and sat down. Something caused him to look up and he caught the eye of the man at the other table, openly staring. Simms nodded. "Mighty hot, isn't it?"

"You're not a bounty hunter," the man said, his voice graveled and low, "so what are you doing here?"

Simms kept his eyes locked on the man's for a moment before turning away, lifting off his hat with both hands, and dusting off the crown. "Passing through, friend. I'll be gone before you know it."

"Is that right?"

"Yes." Simms brought his eyes back to the man's. "It is."

"Looks like you been out on the trail for a long time." He jutted his chin towards Simms's dust-soiled boots. "Travelled far?"

"Colorado River ferry, before that Fort Bridger."

The man whistled. "That *is* quite a way. See any mischief?"

"By that, you mean Indians?"

"Them and the Mormons. Hear they're fixing to fight."

Simms nodded. "These are dangerous times."

"Yeah, and dangerous men along with it."

Simms smiled and at that point Martinson appeared, bearing a chipped plate filled with a few hunks of bread, pieces of cheese, and a sliver of over-cooked bacon. He put it down in front of Simms, together with the beer. "Don't mind Tavis," he said, by way of explanation, "he's lived too long on his own to know anything about the niceties of friendly conversation."

"I left friendly behind a long, long time ago," grumbled Tavis, settling back in his chair and returning his hat to its former position.

Simms sampled the food, placing some of the bacon on the bread and laying slices of cheese on top. He took a huge bite then washed it down with the beer.

Martinson shuffled his feet. "Mind if I join you?"

Simms, mouth full, shook his head and indicated for the man to sit. He took another bite.

"We don't often get strangers here, not nowadays."

Simms drank, swallowed and dabbed at his mouth with the serviette Martinson had supplied. "Your other customers certainly didn't take kindly to my arrival."

"They're some of Greenfield Smith's boys, most of them of questionable parentage and tarnished backgrounds." He laughed. "They often wander in, play their card games, then leave. Rarely do they spend more money than they need to."

"They don't get drunk you mean?"

"Greenfield is a temperance man, Mister… What did you say your name was?"

"Simms." They shook hands.

"Nice to meet you, Mister Simms, but as I was saying, Greenfield does not take kindly to his employees partaking of the drink, not to any degree, if you get my meaning. As his is the biggest working ranch in these parts, and therefore the biggest employer, his boys tend to do as they are told."

"I'm hoping to ride over to Bovey a little later."

"Bovey?" Martinson chewed his lip, considering Simms words. "There's not much there these days. Used to be a town of over two thousand souls, now it has little more than five hundred, and most of those of the undesirable kind."

"It has a hotel?"

"Two or three, of sorts. I know the owner of the best one. Ellis Stoker. A good man, if a little gruff."

Simms bit off another piece of bread. "What does gruff mean?"

"He has the patience of a rattler, that's what I'm saying. He's just as mean, too. It's the reason he's survived for so long, but business is non-existent nowadays, like everywhere else in this God-forsaken Territory. I reckon in a few more years, maybe less, it'll be a ghost town."

"Must have been a lot different when the gold rush was on."

"No comparison! Damn, there were times when I had to squeeze people in here with a crowbar." He laughed, stretching out his legs. "It's good to have someone to talk to, for a change."

Simms raised his glass, drank, smacked his lips. "You still keep provisions here? I need a few things. Grain, for my horse." He studied the last piece of cheese on his plate. "Powder, balls and caps."

"I can make up some paper cartridges, if that will help." Martinson waited. Simms merely nodded.

Tavis sat upright, pushing his hat back and blew out a long breath. "Who in the hell are you, mister?"

Both Simms and Martinson glanced towards the man before Simms said, "Fifty-two calibre, for my Hall-North. I know they're not usual, but I'd—"

"I think I might have some," said Martinson. "That's a fine weapon."

"Yes it is. You know about guns?"

"Some. Many of the miners passing through were ex-soldiers, from the Mexican War."

The seconds dragged out. Simms popped the last piece of cheese into his mouth. "I might need some other bits and pieces."

"My store is out back," said Martinson, jerking his thumb behind him. "It's secure and dry. Most of my stock goes back some, but it's all sound, I can promise you that."

"Expensive too, I'll bet."

Tavis barked out a laugh. "He's got you figured there, Benjie!"

"Shut your mouth, Tavis," snarled Martinson, but his anger was a sham as his face split into a broad grin. He shrugged. "My full name is Benjamin Forest Martinson. At least, it is since my landing in this land of opportunity some years back. I kept my family name, but the rest is Americanized."

"You came for the gold?"

"Like I said, to sell supplies to the miners. I figured I could make more doing that than panning my life away looking for something which was no longer there." He folded his arms. "Where you from?"

"Illinois."

Martinson whistled. "God-damn, that's the other side of the world. Illinois? Shit."

"Went to Illinois once," said Tavis. "Chicago. Mighty big city."

"What the hell were you doing in Chicago, Tavis?"

"Business."

Martinson chuckled, "Whoring is what you mean."

"I come originally from up near Huron," continued Tavis, "heard of the gold, made my way west and thought I'd spend a little time in the Windy City on the way. Got into a fight, lost most of my grub-stake and fell in with two characters who were making their way here also." He shook his head. "Those two wayward bastards gone and died on me before we got even halfway. The rest is history."

Martinson cleared his throat. "Tavis here used to be sheriff."

Simms' mouth fell open. "You had a sheriff here?"

"We had a church, saloon, some twenty or so homesteads. Even Wells Fargo were thinking of opening an office here. It was not long after we elected Tavis that most of the place was burned down. Some said it was arson, some said it was Tavis." He chuckled again. "Most said it was some asshole clearing brushwood from his land that set the whole thing to light. Me and my wife cut a wind break, saved this place, but not much else was left after the flames died down."

"That's a helluva story," said Simms shaking his head and looked across at Tavis. "So, you were out of a job."

"Within a month. People just packed up and went, except for Greenfield Smith, of course. His ranch had the monopoly on the land and within a year he owned every spread there ever was."

"Convenient."

"Yes. It surely was."

"Meaning?"

Tavis didn't speak. Instead, he brushed his knees and stood up, repositioning his hat. "What did you say you did, mister?"

Simms smiled. "I didn't. But, if you're interested, I'm a detective. Of the Pinkerton Detective Agency, out of Chicago, Illinois."

"Holy Mother and Joseph," spluttered Tavis. "What in the name of God is a Pinkerton Detective?"

"My job."

Tavis pulled a face, shot a glance at Martinson, and stood up. "Like I say, a regulator. Them Mormon folk, they've lived their lives without any interference from us, but as soon as some asshole over in Washington decides they don't like people doing their own thing, they get all high and mighty. This is only the beginning, trust me when I say it."

"Well, I'm not from Washington," said Simms, "and I'm not here to cause trouble with the Mormons, although I do suspect trouble is coming." He looked at Martinson. "There are soldiers at the Colorado River ferry. There's already been some gunplay, but no one was hurt."

"You've ranged far, mister."

"Yes I have."

Tavis muttered something under his breath and strode out without another word.

Martinson sighed. "He gets nervous around lawmen. I think it has more to do with his past than who he is now."

"So, this is all there is around here, and Bovey too. Both dying towns."

"Yes, that's about it. I can't see things ever picking up again, lest they find more gold, but I highly doubt that. The only growth industry here is cattle."

Simms nodded and pushed his finished plate away. He drank down his beer and Martinson took the hint, scooped up the glass and returned to the counter to fill it up again. He came back, put the refilled glass down in front of Simms and sat. "There is another cattle man, name of Pilcher, a little to the east. Not half as big as Greenfield Smith, but a fine man. He also built a town and I've heard it prospers."

"Pilcher is dead."

Martinson stopped, mouth falling open. "What did you say? *Dead*? How, what happened?"

"Gunned down by the two men I'm hunting. I've been scouring the whole of this territory for them. From what I gather, they made their way to Bovey."

"Pilcher's dead," Martinson repeated in a low voice, shaking his head. "He was a good man, Pilcher was, well respected. What the hell did they kill him for?"

"They kill just about anything that comes their way. They shot the local animal-doctor too, almost killed his sister—"

"Cathy? Oh sweet Jesus, is she all right?"

Simms shrugged. "Not sure. They sent for a doctor, a surgeon I believe. She has a bullet lodged in her head, pressing down on her brain. She's numb, all down one side, but she's still breathing."

"Good God Almighty. I'll take a wander over to the ranch. Old man Greenfield Smith said he was putting up telegraph lines, so I'll check, see if there is anything I can find out. If you're planning on going over to Bovey, sounds as if you might be going up against two mean individuals."

"I am," said Simms, smiled and quietly finished his beer.

Twenty-eight

Her name was Noreen and she sat on the buckboard with her face set straight ahead, her vision blurred by the tears she shed.

The nag trundled on, head down, resolved to its constant burden of pulling the wagon. But Noreen paid the animal little heed and when it keeled over and died on the ground, she sat down beside it and knew her own death was close. She drank the last of her water that same morning and studied Mason's Navy Colt, wondering if she should end it now.

She stood after a long, long time and trudged to the rear of the wagon to take a look inside, the first time she had done so since leaving Bovey. She found a collection of cooking utensils, clothes and blankets. Some were blood-stained, but there was nothing of any use, nothing to relieve her situation so she hung her head, realizing this was the end of her trail.

The first warning she had of their approach was a tiny rumbling, like the sound of distant thunder, emanating from the ground. She straightened and turned, half expecting to see Newhart and Mason bearing down on her like something out of Revelations.

But the riders who approached were not Newhart and Mason, they were something far worse.

Four of them, dressed in threadbare shirts of various colors. Their legs bare, from below the knee they wore deerskin or buffalo boots.

One held a rifle, the others bows. They looked ravaged, stick thin, but their flesh gleamed like bronze in the sun.

They reigned in their ponies and stood in silence, watching her.

She held the Colt by her side but made no move to bring it up, knowing it would be the last thing she would do. The one with the rifle jumped down from his pony and came closer. He was almost the same size as her, a small man, deep creases in his burnished face, but eyes as clear as the sky, revealing a keen intelligence. He stared into her eyes for a moment before he leaned past and put his head into the wagon. He grunted and stood upright again. He said something to the others, which she couldn't understand, before he repeated the same words directly to her. She frowned and he raised his voice, louder this time, as if angry. Before she could offer up any form of reply, he shot out his hand and grabbed the pistol. He held it up and called to one of his companions, who dropped from his mount and came over. She gazed at him, his shirt open, his body taut, hard-muscled. Amazingly, he smiled at her before he took the gun, checked it, and made some positive grunts from the back of his throat.

The first Indian said something to her again but again she frowned, shook her head, and then his hand slowly came out and folded around her breast. She knew what would happen next and she sank within herself.

The second one lifted her in his arms and laid her gently down in the back of the wagon. She did not resist, knowing death would swiftly follow, and tried her best to empty her mind as each of them took her in turns amongst the clothes and the blankets. When they had finished, they swaggered back to their ponies, drunk with their lust. One of them gave her an animal skin gourd full of water, which he placed next to her naked body. She barely knew what he was doing. He reached out and stroked her cheek. He then clambered outside and rejoined his companions.

She lay there, staring up at the canvas roof of the wagon, her mind a blank. She was vaguely aware of them outside, whooping and laughing but paid them no mind, until the first gunshot rang out across the prairie. Everything changed then and she sat bolt upright, drawing up her knees to cover her breasts, uncontrolled trembling overcoming her. It had to be Mason and the thought was a terrifying one.

Another gunshot and one of the natives screamed. Noreen took a deep breath and edged towards the entrance to the wagon and dared to peek between the flaps of the tent. Two of them were on the ground, one of them still, the other, the leader with the rifle, rolling around, moaning in agony. The remaining two were pulling themselves across the backs of their ponies when a rider came thundering across the plain. A lone man, like no other she had ever seen. The Indians were screaming, trying to turn their bows towards the devil bearing down upon them, but the ponies were wild, kicking, bucking, sensing the danger, mad with fear. Arrows flew ineffectively through the acrid air, either veering off in various directions or falling short. The man jumped down from his horse, hit the ground at a run, swerving this way and that, to take up a position behind some large rocks. He held two handguns.

The Indians fought to control their ponies, kicking their flanks, yanking hard on the reins. Noreen watched it all playing out before her from the safety of the wagon, a curious, detached series of images. She saw the natives turning their ponies, readying themselves to gallop off, watched the man rear up from behind the rocks, first left hand, then the right pointing straight, working the hammers of his guns, firing off shot after shot. The breeze whipped around his coat, his face in shadow, but she knew it was not Mason and the thought brought lightness to her heart, despite the horrors she witnessed. She saw him shoot both the natives many times and when the young one who stroked her cheek fell, she cared not a jot. Soon they all lay motionless on the ground, a stillness falling, preternatural, unearthly.

After a moment, the man strode forward towards the leader, whose head rolled from side to side, and put a bullet in his brain. That was the end of it and he paused, slipping one gun into its holster then reloading the other. He looked up and their eyes met.

Noreen clamped a hand across her mouth and fell back into the wagon.

Mason. Indians. And now this other devil. What had she done to deserve such treatment, to be punished this way, to lose everything she had? She did not believe she could take any more and she scrambled around wildly, looking for a weapon, anything to defend herself with. When the wagon flaps ripped open, she yelped, arms across her breasts, eyes blazing and she waited for this demon to do what all the rest did.

The stranger smiled and handed her a blanket. "Don't be afraid, miss, not anymore. They're dead. Get dressed, then we'll talk."

* * *

Simms made coffee in an iron pot on the fire. He'd dragged the bodies some way off and set them aflame, freeing the ponies to gallop off across the range. He looked up when she emerged from the wagon, hair combed, dress as smooth as she could make it. She smiled and he spread out a blanket so she could sit.

He handed her a cup, which she clasped in both palms.

"I never said thank you."

Simms shrugged. "I reckon I arrived too late for thanks. At first, I didn't know what was happening. I saw them around the wagon, but I had no idea what they had done."

"But you killed them anyway."

"They wouldn't be up to discussing the niceties."

"There were none."

"That I can believe." He drank his coffee. "I'm heading for Bovey."

"Dear God, I just came from there."

He looked at her. "From Bovey? When?"

"A couple of days ago. We were fixing on leaving, my husband and I, but as it was, events sort of conspired against us." She turned her face towards the smoldering pile of bodies. "As they often do. I was delayed."

"Your husband? Where is he now?"

"Back at Bovey. My husband Joss and his brother, Niles. They're both dead."

"I'm sorry to hear that. Was it Indians again?"

"No." She looked into her coffee cup. "I don't know who you are, mister, or what you want, but I'm grateful for what you've done. Every man I've met since Joss and Niles died, they have sort of tested my faith in humankind. You've begun to rebuild it, I think."

"It'll take some rebuilding, I believe."

She looked at him, her eyes wet with tears. "I've kept it hidden, way down in my guts. If I think about it too much, I'll go crazy."

"Then don't think of it. What's done is done, and you're still alive. Hold on to that."

"But in the dead of night, sometimes the memories, they come and…" She shivered, drank some coffee and stared into the fire. "And now those savages, what they did… They weren't violent in any way, but even so …"

"This is a brutal land, miss. I can't begin to understand why you are out here, all alone."

"It's as I said, we were fixing to leave, but something happened. I had to leave alone. I had no choice. Maybe if I had stopped to think it through I would have stayed at Bovey, but… perhaps not. Bovey is not the place it was, not since the gold ran out."

"They say there are other seams, that it will surge up again, in other areas."

"Maybe so. You hear all sorts of stories, but I no longer care one way or the other. Are you a miner?"

"I'm a detective, from out of Chicago. I came to find a young woman, kidnapped by two men. I've been on their trail for way too long, and now it's taking me to Bovey."

"Two men?"

He noted her tone and saw the pain in her face, the remnants of something awful. "As you came from Bovey, it might be you may have seen them." He pulled out the wanted poster and smoothed it out in front of her and for a long time she stared at it in silence.

"Newhart and Mason," she said quietly. "These are the men you are after."

"Yes." He tapped the amount of the reward. "I reckon this has gone up quite a lot since this was first posted. They've been shooting their way across the Territory ever since they took Miss Randall."

"Miss Randall?"

"The girl, Elisabeth Randall, the daughter of General Randall, late of the Mexican War. I found her, thank God, safe and well and took her to Fort Bridger. With any luck she'll be making her way east to be reunited with her father." He folded up the poster and returned it to his inside pocket. "There's a town, more of a settlement really, close to the Greenfield Smith ranch. We'll stick to the trail and it will lead us straight to it."

"Us? You mean…"

"You can't be out here on your own, miss, and I do not think you wish to return to Bovey. So, I'll escort you if I may. It's a day's ride, somewhat less. Once there, I'll hand you over to a man named Martinson, a good man. There you can rest up, try and put all of this behind you."

"What will you do?"

"I shall go to Bovey and end this once and for all."

"And kill them? Those animals?"

Simms frowned. He did not wish to press her over what may or may not have happened, but if she had any information that might help him, then he needed to know. He took a slow breath. "Something happened at Bovey, didn't it?"

"The man on your poster, the one called Mason. He shot them dead. Joss and Niles. Shot them with no more regard than if they were rattlesnakes. Then he attempted to have his way with me, but I resisted. Nevertheless, I can still feel his hot, stinking breath on my cheeks." She looked away, perhaps from shame, perhaps from fear. "I hit him over the head with an empty bottle, which didn't break, unfortunately.

I wanted to kill him." She balled her hands up into tight fists. "Instead, I ran. Stole their wagon, and ran."

"If you'd stayed, he would have ended up killing you."

"I would have been better off, given what has happened. I've lost everything."

"Well, listen, you've done nothing wrong, miss, it's not your—"

"Noreen. My name is Noreen."

"Noreen. As I was saying, it's not your fault any of this happened. You have a duty to stay alive, a God-given right to be safe. I'll escort you to Martinson's, where you can begin to put all of this behind you. I'll make sure no harm will come to you."

Her eyes grew wide. "You'd do that for me?"

"Yes, of course. It's my job."

"I think it's more than your job which makes you do such things, mister. But whatever it is, I thank you, with all my heart."

"Then gather whatever you have. You can get up behind me, sleep if you can. For you, at least, these horrors are over."

She smiled, took his hand and kissed it. And Simms stared at his hand and swallowed down the sob threatening to gurgle out of his throat.

Twenty-nine

Martinson came out of his store at a run, catching the woman around the waist and easing her to the ground. He shook his head. "Those two animals did this?"

"Them, and other things." Simms jumped down from the buckboard and together the two men took the unconscious Noreen into one of the outbuildings behind the store. Inside one was a makeshift bedroom, with a rickety dressing-table, wash bowl, and small mirror. They laid her down on the bed.

"You had all this ready?"

Martinson grunted. "My wife, she…" He shrugged.

Simms patted him gently on the shoulder and, before anything more was said, pressed a five-dollar bill into the man's hand. Martinson frowned. "Until I get back, feed her, make sure she rests. She's been through a lot."

Both men went back outside and Simms walked over to the wagon and unhitched his horse. "I have another animal," said Martinson. "She's young, but tough. I'll keep yours here until you return."

"I'm grateful, Martinson." He reached inside his coat for more money, but Martinson shook his head. Simms smiled briefly. "The trail is getting more dangerous by the day. Indians are starving, becoming desperate. If I were you, Martinson…" He let the words drift away.

Martinson grunted. "I hear you. I've lived here all these years and never once had any bad dealings with the natives."

"Well, you might now. Keep your wits about you, and get a word to Garfield Smith to do the same."

"I already been to his place, to try that telegraph again. He wasn't there, left behind an old man and his wife to keep the house in order." He pushed his hat to the back of his head. "They told me some things, mister. Some things I did not want to hear."

Simms pulled in a breath, bracing himself for the news he had been dreading.

"Cathy died, mister. The surgeon, he did his best, but... Seems like the bullet, it..." He shook his head. "Seems like the doctor, on his way back to Salt Lake, called in to the ranch, told old man Smith about what happened and how the killers have moved across to Bovey. That's where Smith has gone, to kill those two varmints."

"Or get himself killed. Jesus." He gritted his teeth and looked out across the plain. "Everything I touch, everything I see, withers and dies."

"Mister, it ain't your fault those bastards did what they did." He looked back at the outbuilding and the woman resting inside. "She's might pretty. I'll make sure she's well looked after. Old man Tavis has a Mexican woman who keeps his house, I'll ask him for her help."

"That would be for the best. What those Indians did to her..." He shook his head. "I'm going to end this. When I come back, this place is going to be very different, Martinson. Safe."

"I pray to God you're right."

"Praying ain't got nothing to do with it." He patted the butt of his handgun across his belly. "Mr. Samuel Colt has." Then, together with Martinson, he trudged towards the stable and the new horse waiting for him there.

* * *

He rode through the day and all through the night. As the next morning dawned, he slowed his horse down to a canter and when he found high ground, with rocks and overhanging trees clinging between the cracks, he camped, resting his horse under what shade he could find. He stretched himself out and tried to sleep, but images of Cathy sitting in her wheelchair, trying so hard to smile, haunted him and finally he sat up, rubbing his face hard. But the images remained and he cursed this land for all its brutality and excess. One day, law would hold sway over the entire Territory, perhaps even further, but for now he must do what he could to overcome the lawlessness, the dangers, the casual violence visited upon so many. He had not known love for so long, he believed it to be forever lost to him. Then he saw Cathy and something stirred from deep inside, and now she was gone. Such thoughts only reinforced his belief that happiness and affection were not for him. He stood, holding the small of his back as he stretched, and gathered up his meagre belongings.

Wary of pushing his horse too hard, he decided to take the remainder of his journey more slowly, but some hours later, the first sounds of distant gunfire changed his mind. He checked his weapons then broke into a steady trot, heading directly towards the sound of battle.

Bovey sat like a sad, downtrodden thing, its buildings dull grey, the streets deserted. From his vantage point, peering through the telescope, he saw the distant puffs of smoke, followed some seconds later by the sharp crack of gunfire. He slowly moved the eyepiece along the main street, looking at either side and sighed. He put the scope away with an angry snap and stood up. Leading his horse by the reins, he carefully made his way down the slight incline, not wishing to draw undue attention to himself.

On the outskirts of the town, he tied his horse up to the hitching rail outside a dilapidated news office, which had not seen life for some considerable time. He was in a side street and from here, the gun shots were more audible, a steady dialogue of blasts. He stepped up onto the boardwalk, and keeping himself close to the front walls of the buildings, he inched his way along towards the end of the street. When he got there, he went down on one knee and eased out his revolver. He took a quick glance up the main street.

Halfway down, from a broken hotel opposite, gun smoke and flashes belched out of a lower window. He saw two bodies on the street, face down, splayed out in the grim attitude of death. He pulled back behind the corner and looked up to the sky. It had to be them holed up in the hotel – Newhart and Mason – but who was attacking them, he could not be sure. He checked his revolver again and made his decision.

Simms sprinted across the street, keeping low, and slammed himself up against the wall of a hardware store, adjacent to where Newhart and Mason fired their weapons through the window. He glared across the street and saw the others, about four or five men sheltering behind an upturned wagon and some cracked, splintered barrels. He held out his right hand, palm forward when they noticed him. They gawped in surprise but seemed to understand he was not their enemy. Simms released a long sigh of relief, stabbed his finger at his chest two or three times, then pointed to the entrance of the hardware store. One of the men nodded and put a shot through the hotel door by way of agreement.

Beyond the men, from the shattered downstairs windows of an abandoned assayer's office, Simms noticed a figure moving inside, the gleaming white of a ten-gallon hat acting like a beacon. Whoever it was poked the barrel of a musket through the broken glass. "We got you covered!" said the person, voice thick with anger. Whoever it was discharged their piece towards the hotel and Simms went through the door of the hardware store at a dash.

The room was dark and damp, shutters melded together by rusted hinges, daylight a foreigner here. Simms screwed up his eyes, trying to make out some of the interior features, and slowly, as he grew accustomed to the gloom, he made out shapes and features. The room was a total mess, ransacked, boxes and crates spilling out across the floor, shelving, tins and cartons smashed. There was nothing of any use here, but Simms was not seeking merchandise. He groped forward, careful not to cut his legs, or trap himself amongst the many pieces of twisted wire and large hunks of jagged wood, hyphenated by rusting nails.

He reached the rear of the store without incident. Here, the debris was less, and a crack in the window gave some light, helping him to gain his bearings. A rickety staircase ran up from his right. He ignored this and went straight to the rear door. He tried to push it open, but it wouldn't budge, so he holstered his firearm and set to slamming his shoulder against the woodwork. It creaked and groaned under this assault but otherwise remained solid. He bit his lip, looked to the window and forced back the twin shutters, which screamed on their rusted hinges. Part of the left pane was missing and he tested the remainder with his fingers, felt the glass giving in the frame. Relieved, he went back into the main room and picked up one of the larger pieces of wood, and set to smashing away the entire window until, at last, he managed to create a hole big enough for him to crawl through. He knocked out the last remaining pieces of jagged glass before searching around the debris for something else.

Gunfire from out front broke his concentration, but only for a moment He continued with his search until he found what he sought over in one of the corners, sticking out from under a pile of discarded, wrecked boxes. A tarpaulin, ripped in numerous places, but otherwise suitable enough for his needs. He took it over to the broken window and laid the thick material across the bottom part of the frame, covering any remaining shards of glass. Satisfied, he stepped back and was about to wriggle through the opening when the front door to the store burst open. Simms whirled, hands outstretched. Several figures filled the doorway. He couldn't tell if this was Mason and his partner, come to snuffle out his out-flanking move, or some of the assailants from across the street.

The one in the lead stepped forward. "Just you hold on one goddamned fucking minute there, boy!"

Simms didn't move. The others stepped through the debris, cursing as they twisted ankles, crushed bottles, none of them moving with the same caution Simms had only moments before.

The lead figure rammed a gun barrel into Simms's guts. "You better speak real quick and tell us who you are, mister."

So Simms took a deep breath and told them everything.

Thirty

From the second-story window, Mason had a good view of the street. Earlier that morning, as he and Newhart scoured the nearby buildings, he'd come across a few weapons. He discarded most, but the Enfield musket seemed sound enough. He had six shots and had already discharged four of them. Two of the men who had attacked them earlier were dead, which brought him some comfort, but he knew time was not on his side. From below, Newhart blazed away with his six-shooter, keeping whoever the rest of those bastards were at bay, but Mason knew the time had come to break free and get away from this murderous place as soon as possible. But in order to do that, they needed horses. The attackers had horses, but how to get to them?

Movement across the street caught his eye and he spotted one of them racing across the street. He moved quick, as if he knew what he was doing. Mason brought the musket up to his eye, but too late, the man was already out of sight. He cursed and spat through the window. He called down, "Newhart, they're trying to get around us. Keep yourself alert now, you hear?"

"I hear you," came the gruff reply from downstairs.

Mason suspected Newhart was drunk, having found more bottles of whisky crated up in an old warehouse two blocks down the street. He cursed again, went to spit out of the window for a second time and saw a bunch of cowboys bursting out into the open. He took a bead on one and dropped him with a well-aimed shot to the upper body. Grinning like a child on Christmas morning, Mason drew back and reloaded the musket with the last round. Another quick look outside, then he scrambled away, running down the stairs to find Newhart slumped against the wall beside the window, gun on his lap, half-empty whisky bottle in his other hand.

"You stupid son of a bitch!"

"Fuck you, Mason. We're gonna die here, so best go out happy, yeah?"

Mason moved over to the window, scanning each side of the street. "Listen to me, they're gonna come through the back. We have to make a break for it."

"Fuck you."

Mason cuffed him across the face and Newhart wailed like a baby. "What you do that for?"

"Shut up, goddamn you!" He wrenched the bottle from his friend's grasp and hurled it away into the far corner. It smashed against the wall, whiskey spraying out in all directions.

"Shit, Mason, you needn't have done that." Newhart sobbed and pressed the back of his hand against his nose.

"We're breaking out; you hear me? We make it across the street, get their horses and go."

"You gotta be kidding me. They'll kill us."

"They'll kill us for sure if we stay here."

"But we have no things. We need water, food."

"We ain't got the time. We have to move now, and hope they have supplies in their saddle bags."

Mason leaned across his friend and squinted into the open. He could see three tethered horses on the far side of the opposite building, but he couldn't make out if there were saddlebags and bedrolls harnessed to their flanks. He cursed. He could spend the rest of the day trying to find essential supplies and he didn't have the luxury of time. He felt sure only minutes remained before they came through the rear entrance, guns blazing.

"We run down to them horses," he said. "We ride, and we don't stop."

"I can't do it, Mason. I feel sick."

Mason glared at him. "You sorry piece of shit. I've a good mind to leave you here, you bastard."

"Do it, Mason. Do it. I can't go on, I truly can't."

Mason cocked his fist, preparing to ram it into his friend's face. Newhart winced, pulled away and Mason blew out his breath hard through his nose. He lowered his fist. "No, I got a better idea." He took a few deep breaths. "You cover me. I'm gonna get to the horses, bring them back here, then we go. You be ready for me, Newhart, because I won't be hanging around for too long. Take this," he handed him the musket. "It has one more round left. Make sure it's a good one."

"I'm gonna be sick," Newhart moaned, ignoring the proffered weapon.

"Well do it quick, then get your sights on the street."

Mason got up just as Newhart turned his head and vomited.

"Goddamn you, Newhart. Don't you fuck this up!"

Newhart moaned and Mason broke out of the hotel without comment. He ran across the street at an acute angle, making straight for the horses. There were the two men behind the overturned wagon who, taken by surprise at Mason's emergence, took a moment to recover and brought up their guns to open up a fusillade of shots.

Mason continued to run, bent double, right arm held out towards the wagon, spacing his shots, not looking, all of his concentration on the horses. Bullet whizzed over his head and when he hit the boardwalk to the right of the two men, a shot smacked into the wooden slats at his feet. He swore at his lack of cover, dropped to one knee, reloading his revolver as quickly as he could manage.

Mason glanced up. The two men approached, keeping up a steady fire. Each held two guns, alternating from left hand to right, to fire at Mason's frame, a tempting target as anyone could hope.

His ears rang with the gunfire, but Mason worked calmly and methodically, pushed home the last percussion cap, eased back the hammer, took careful aim and shot the first man in the chest. He dropped, a look of abject surprise on his face. The other man swore, fired wildly, and Mason shot him, once in the stomach and then, as the man folded up double, hit him square on the top of his head.

"Damned cowboys," swore Mason, "why the hell don't you learn to shoot?" He swung around and stomped off towards the horses. They shied away from him, nostrils flaring, snorting out their breath. Mason did his best to calm them with low, soothing noises but as he loosened their reins, one of them bucked away, tearing itself loose from his grip, and galloped away down the street. Desperate now, Mason took hold of the remaining horse's bridle with both hands, repeating soft cooing noises over and over and swung himself up into the saddle. The animal whickered and stomped its feet. Mason hit the horse's rump with his hat and it took flight, pounding towards the hotel.

Newhart was in the doorway, his face the color of urine as Mason reined in the horse before him, fighting hard to keep the animal under control. "Are you kidding me?"

"Get the hell up on this saddle, you asshole," Mason screamed, struggling with the horse as it kicked out, causing plumes of dust to rise up from the hard, arid earth. Newhart went into convulsions, violent coughing ripping through his body.

"Move yourself!"

Newhart threw away the musket and groped forward, hand outstretched, Mason took it, and lifted him off his feet just as men came racing through the hotel. They were shouting, setting off a blaze of bullets, most of which caused no harm to their intended targets out in the street, locked in a desperate battle with the maddened horse.

Mason groaned with the effort of lifting his friend onto the back of the horse. Newhart clung on, trying to get his leg over the horse's rump, but the animal was out of control and it broke into a wild stampede. "Shit, Mason!"

They stormed down the street, Newhart holding on, one hand around the saddle cantle, the other gripping Mason's forearm. Mason kept his face forward, straining to keep the horse under control. His throat was closed, as dry as the ground, and the sweat poured down from his brow, stinging his eyes, but he knew he must not stop. Bullets trailed red hot through the air, and he heard the men shouting, cursing, damning him to hell and back. But he kept going, aware of Newhart struggling to pull himself onto the horse.

And then, all of a sudden, he made it, managing to wrap his arms around Mason's waist. They both leaned forward, allowing the animal to race forward unchecked and soon the distance between themselves and the town of Bovey broadened and they were free.

Late in the afternoon, confident no one was pursuing them, they stopped and found a space amongst the rocks to throw themselves on the ground and lie still, to take stock and try to reassemble their confused minds.

After longer than he wanted, Mason sat up and rubbed his hands through his hair. "Shit, we've got nothing. No water, food, bullets. Nothing."

"We left in kind of a hurry, Mason." Newhart remained on the ground, eyes closed. He wore a filthy white shirt and dust covered pants. His black boots were grey with grime. "I reckon we wait here awhile, ambush the bastards when they come, then use their own supplies to replenish ourselves."

"I do believe that is the first, genuinely sensible thing you have ever said, Newhart."

"Thank you kindly."

Mason lifted himself to his feet and peered out across the plain. "We have got a good spot here, but what if they don't come?"

"Well, then we'll have to head west, try and make for another town."

"What if there ain't no more towns? What then?"

"Mason, we have to do something. We can't just stay here and die."

Mason tried to spit but his mouth was so dry all he managed was as strangulated croak. He looked at the horse, blown and sweating. "I got an idea," he said.

"I hope it's a good one."

"I believe it is," and he slowly drew his revolver.

* * *

Simms stood in the street, looking towards the direction Mason and Newhart took.

"They'll be heading over to Martinson's I shouldn't wonder," said the large, grizzled older man who stepped up alongside him. "It's the only place there is before Salt Lake."

"And that is way too far," added another; a lean, muscular cowboy. "To cross that prairie on one horse," he shook his head. "Nope, the only place they can get to is Martinson's."

"We'll ride with you," said the older man, "and finish this."

"No," said Simms. He nodded down the street. "Bury your men, Mr. Smith. I'll set off down the trail on my own. It took me less than two days to cross from Martinson's to here, reckon I'll take longer on the way back, but I'll run them down, have no fear."

"You have resolve, mister, I'll say that for you."

"I have one thing which gives me the motivation to kill those two sons of bitches, and nothing else." Simms readjusted his hat. "Retribution."

Thirty-one

He picked up their trail with ease, the weight of the two men causing the horse's hooves to sink deep in the compacted ground. Leaning across his saddle, he walked slowly on, pausing every few moments to drink from his canteen. The sun beat down with a greater intensity than it had since he arrived in this blighted land, all those hundreds of years ago. He wondered if his office back in Chicago had the slightest notion what this assignment had cost and the more he dwelt on the idea, the more he considered changing his personal direction. He'd fought long and hard these past twenty or so years, and he doubted if a single year had gone by without him killing someone. It was not the life he wanted, nor wished to continue. One last effort, one last moment of killing. Then it must stop. All of it.

On the second day, he came across the carcass of a horse. It was virtually a shell, drained of all its goodness. He'd seen this before, back in the war, when men had killed their horses and drunk the blood. A man could survive for days on such sustenance. In three days, those two bastards would make Martinson's store.

And the woman who sought shelter there. Noreen.

The one good point, he knew, was that now the men he pursued were on foot. Their progress would be slower. He would be on them within twenty-four hours.

Later that same day he spotted two figures making their sorry way across the open range. He got down from his horse and took out the telescope.

There were two of them, but they were not Newhart and Mason. The man on the lead horse pulled a sled fashioned out of buffalo hide and twigs. Behind, walking at a steady, even pace, was a woman. Indians. They were veering off the trail, heading for an area of scrub and bracken, which seemed to offer shelter from the searing heat. Simms picked out the remnants of an old camp close by. Simms put the telescope away and gnawed at his lip. He should leave them to it, concentrate on his quarry.

But then he saw the tell-tale puffs of dust way over to his left and knew that circumstances were coming together to offer him the opportunity to bring this whole, sorry affair to an end.

He turned his telescope to the dust, to make sure, and hissed, his mouth curling into a grin.

It was them, Newhart and Mason. Even at this distance, he knew they could be no one else. They looked bedraggled and forlorn, walking as if asleep, with no idea their demise was so close.

He quickly gathered what he needed, checking his carbine. It was a fine weapon, had served him well, but now it would be called upon to do its greatest service. Shouldering it, he led his horse over to a clump of rocks, which sprouted from the desert like ancient, abandoned monuments. From there, he could make his way out of sight of the two desperadoes, find a good vantage point, and kill them. Chivalric thoughts played no part in his plans. Throughout the campaigns against Mexico, Simms would often find escape from the horrors through the reading of literature, a fact that did little to convince his commanding officers he had the stomach for the real fight. He proved them wrong, time and time again, but his love of reading never faltered. Until now. For the deaths and suffering of others brought him to the conclusion that the world of imagination was no barrier to reality. Reality would always win through, so he accepted it, embraced killing as a grim necessity and put all thoughts of mercy and conscience out of his mind.

He left his horse out of sight and hobbled. He relieved the animal of the saddle and placed it close by on the ground. He needed his horse fresh for when he delivered the bodies to Martinson.

Edging his way between the rocks, he took what he hoped was a parallel route to that of Mason and Newhart. He kept himself out of sight, judging the direction through skill and intuition, scrambling as quickly and as quietly as he could over the scorching stones.

When he finally managed to inch his way to a promontory, which overlooked the ancient campsite, he flattened himself against the rock, levelled the carbine, and waited.

Thirty-two

They called him Wide Eagle, but that was long ago, before the hunger struck and his people starved. Now, they may just as well have called him Small Eagle, or Bone Eagle, for his clothes hung as if made for a man twice his size. His ribs protruded from skin thin as paper, the flesh grey and sickly. He could not recall the last time he had eaten. And the lack of water withered him. The land, which once nurtured and sustained him, was now his enemy. Barren and cruel. He sat, perched on a rocky outcrop, peering out across the dusty plain, but lost in thought. The hours, like the view, blurred into one and he knew, if he knew nothing at all, no game would wander into sight. Nothing lived here now, nothing ever would again. At least, not whilst he breathed.

He pulled himself upright, stretching both arms above his head, the single shot rifle he'd stripped from a corpse some days before helping him achieve more leverage. One final look across the prairie before he slid down off the rock, turned and tramped away, head down, despondent.

If he had waited one more minute, he would have seen the rider appearing on the horizon. From this distance, he may not have recognized it as a man, perhaps thinking it to be a buffalo, a deer, anything he might shoot, take back to his woman, feed them. But he was unaware, the hunger gnawing at his guts, depression weighing him down, growing heavier with each step.

His woman looked up from the fire she was making in the remains of the deserted camp they found, surrounded by the carcasses of eaten dogs, ghosts of children lying in the dirt, a tiny abandoned moccasin, a broken doll fashioned out of a twisted piece of wood. He answered her hopeful look with a single shake of his head, led his horse over to a piece of scrub, and tethered it to a twig. He ran his hand gently over its flank, the ribs protruding through the thin flesh. This was the last one, the sole survivor from a time when the tribe would ride out on hunting parties, a band of twenty or more armed warriors, whooping with expectation, thrilled with the thought of riding over the plain, of pitching their strength and cunning against the buffalo. On their return, the entire village would greet them, laughing and dancing, the women with their children embracing their menfolk, the aged nodding with pride and quiet appreciation. In those days nobody ever dwelt on what life might become if the rains did not come, if the grass did not grow and the buffalo simply disappeared. Until now, and now it was too late. The world had turned against them, the spirits of the land deserting the tribe, leaving it forlorn, starving and dying.

Wide Eagle leaned on his rifle, struggling not to break down and weep. Nothing but memories remained now, lost in the swirling sand devils, the hard, compacted ground sucked dry. There was no hope here but Wide Eagle, the last of the warriors, was too weak to bundle up his tepee and again set off across the plain in search of game. How long would it be until his strength gave out completely and he rolled himself up into a ball and surrendered to the inevitable? He sniffed loudly, wiped his nose with the back of his hand, and went through the open flap of his tepee, the tepee his woman erected. Where would he be without her?

She came up to him and laid her hand on his shoulder. She appeared hopeful, but when she took in his look of despair, she seemed to crumple within herself. She pushed past him and collapsed on the ground, clutching at her shrunken belly, and moaned with the pain of it all.

"What are we to do," she asked, pulling a thin blanket over shoulders virtually pure bone, the skin so thin, the muscles wasted.

"I shall try again later, before the sun goes down." He slumped down beside her, resting his hand on the hardness of her hip. "We have water; we can last another day or so."

"And if you find nothing. What will we do tomorrow, with our bellies so empty, our bodies so weak? I think we shall die tomorrow."

He looked at her back. She lay on her side, turned away from him, and he knew she was crying. He glanced across to his rifle. He had less than half a dozen shots remaining. If he found nothing by this time tomorrow… He sighed. "Let us not talk of what might or might not be. I may find something later. A prairie dog, maybe. Something."

She did not reply. Her breathing grew deeper and he realized she was already asleep. Weary himself, he snuggled down next to her, her body warm despite it being little more than a sack of bones. Prairie dogs came out at dusk. If the spirits willed it, he may be lucky and catch one before it shot down into its hole in the ground. If there were still animals out there. If…

He sat bolt upright as the shadow fell across him, reaching out for the rifle. The foot came down on his hand and he cried out, tried to twist himself free and the barrel of a big, heavy revolver smacked across the side of his face and he fell back across his wife, who leaped up, screaming.

"Oh now, you shut the fuck up, you crazy squaw."

"Squawking like a squaw," said the second man, laughing at his own wit.

"Like a fucking squawker."

Wide Eagle propped himself up on one arm, his head ringing, the pain lancing through his cheek. He dabbed at the flesh with his hand, and stared at his fingers, red with blood. His wife wrapped her arms around him, both of them backing off into the corner, staring up at the intruders filling their tepee with their threatening bulk.

"You got any food, you pair of squawkers?"

The first man scanned the interior, kicked away a few empty pots, whilst the second covered Wide Eagle and his wife with a revolver.

"Is there anything, Mason?"

"Not a goddamned thing," said Mason, picking up an old rag between finger and thumb and sniffing at it. He curled down his mouth and threw the material away, "There ain't nothing here but the memories of what there once was," he snarled, hitched up his trousers, and stared down at the others. "You are a sorry sight to behold, my good red friend. And as you ain't got no food, I don't really see the point in keeping you alive." He reached for his belt and the revolver stuffed there.

Wide Eagle pressed his wife closer to him as she took up a prolonged, bleating wail. Mason frowned. "Oh my," he said, "you do make some awful strange sounds. But worry not," he pulled out the revolver, "you won't be making 'em for much longer."

"Hey Mason," piped up the second man, chuckling to himself, "before you do that, let's partake of that there squaw. She may not have much on her, but she sure is a pretty little thing."

Mason smiled, "You ain't speaking no lies, Newhart. We'll have our fill of her, then pop 'em both in the pot for supper."

Wild Eagle gritted his teeth, glaring at them. He shot a glance to his rifle, estimating how long it would take him to reach it, turn and shoot. Too long. He'd be dead before he took one step.

"Better still," continued Mason, "let's keep her. We can eat the boy here, keep her fresh for the rest of the journey."

"Damned if you ain't full of good ideas today, Mason."

"I will kill myself first," spat Wide Eagle's wife.

"My oh my," said Mason, the smile spreading wide over his face, "you can both speak English? Where did you learn, boy?"

"Fort Bridger. Please," said Wide Eagle, reaching out one hand, still smeared with the blood from his split cheek, "we have nothing here but ourselves. Let us stay together. We are close to death and we have little hope for—"

"Nah," said Mason, shaking his head, "I'm afraid not, my red friend. We're starving too. This damned country hasn't seen rain for nigh on three months, maybe more, and we ain't seen a single watering hole since we set out from Little Butes some four weeks ago."

"*Little Butes*?" Newhart laughed, shaking his heads. "My God, that seems like a century ago, Mason."

"Maybe it was." Mason shrugged, and jabbed his revolver towards the cowering pair of natives. "But since then, throughout everything, we are now as close to desperate as a man can get. My friend here, he's got a bad leg, can't put much weight on it, and he's suffering worse than most." He eased back the Colt's hammer, pointing the gun directly towards Wide Eagle. "Nothing personal, but we do have to eat."

Wide Eagle closed his eyes, hugged his wife tighter still as she took up wailing once more, and waited for life to end.

"Hold on, Mason."

Wide Eagle opened his eyes. His wife held her breath. Mason snapped his head around towards Newhart, eyes flashing, "What the *fuck* is it now?"

Newhart grinned, "We're gonna have some fun before we dine, I reckon. Let's peg out the little guy so he can watch the show before we put a bullet in his pan."

Mason frowned, "That's sick, Newhart. If I didn't know you better, I'd say you was trying to be like me!"

Newhart giggled. "I think I am, Mason. That's for sure. I miss your nightly moving with little Elisabeth. Man, listening to her moans and groan, that was something else!" He rubbed his face and licked his lips. "I want to see you in action again, taking the squaw. It sure would bring some life to the proceedings, don't you think?"

The wife wailed, Wide Eagle wilted, the fight leaving him, and Mason laughed out loud.

The early evening sun was dipping towards the horizon, casting everything in a warm, golden glow, which might, at any other time, be termed beautiful. But not this evening. Wide Eagle was stripped naked and lashed to a post. They'd put a gag into his mouth, to quell his protests. His wife lay on the ground, also naked, a blanket giving her some relief from the loose shale which otherwise would have cut into her flesh. She was quiet now, the crying long ceased, her eyes locked on the sky.

Wide Eagle stared. He sat perhaps ten or so paces from where the others were. The one called Newhart was cackling endlessly whilst Mason undressed. It took him some time. He wore a greasy, frayed duster coat, thick corduroy trousers, checked shirt and full-length underclothes, as well as his gun and leather belt from which hung a knife in its sheath. He kept a small canvas bag suspended over his shoulder, together with his hat and gun belt and stood, otherwise naked, displaying his erection with a great show of pride.

"Reckon she's gonna enjoy that," said Newhart, nodding in appreciation, drooling.

"I reckon so too," said Mason, lowering himself to his knees. His eyes roamed over the girl's olive skin. Despite her deprivations, her body appeared healthy enough to cause the blood to rush through his loins, making him harder still. Mason licked his lips. "Damn if this wasn't a fine idea of yours, Newhart."

He reached across, placed a hand on each of her knees, and gently eased apart her legs. She did not resist. "My, she may be skinny but she is one beautiful looking gal," said Newhart, standing some way off, clawing at the growing bulge in his own, still-covered crotch. "She is gonna serve you well over the next week or so, I reckon."

"You're damned right," breathed Mason, his voice husky with lust and he eased himself forward.

Newhart wiggled over on his knees to get a better view, pulling open his pants, pulling out his eager, pulsing manhood, lips slack, saliva caught in the sunlight trailing from his mouth, shining like silver threads.

His head erupted in a massive explosion of blood and brain, his body leaving the ground, thrown into the air as if it were as light as tumbleweed, to land some yards away, twitching and hideous.

For a moment, the world froze. Mason gawped, erection collapsing, not believing the evidence of his eyes. His friend and companion, forever supportive, true and constant, now lay a bloody, malformed thing on the ground. For the first time in his life, he sobbed, one single, guttural inhalation of strangled breath. Then he moved.

Everything happened at once. The girl took up a prolonged bout of screaming, tugging at the blanket to cover her quaking body, Wide Eagle kicking and twisting in a wild, desperate effort to free himself from the cords which bound him to the post. And Mason, whirling around, eyes wide, mouth open, scanning the horizon, the distant hillside. Nothing moved, no tell-tale flash of a muzzle, no glint from metal, Nevertheless Mason fired off round after round from his revolver, careless of where he shot, hopeful he might hit the unknown, invisible assailant.

Six shots rang out across the open plain, but nothing stirred, no sign of any living thing. Mason quickly tossed away his spent handgun and delved into the shoulder bag for another. He cursed, checking each cylinder, and realized several were empty. He broke down, the tears cutting tiny trails through the grime covering his face, despair croaking from the back of his throat.

The girl rolled over to where Mason had dropped his clothes. Frantic, she searched through them, found a knife, another, smaller revolver. She eyed Mason as he continued to whimper, then scampered over to where Wild Eagle sat. She put the gun down beside her husband and worked furiously at the ropes binding him with the knife. She grunted with the effort, checking Mason every few seconds over her shoulder.

"Goddamn fucking thing," said Mason through gritted teeth, raising the revolver skyward and shaking it in fury, "Damn you to fucking hell!" He looked across to girl, saw her trying to free her man, and took a step forward just as the heavy bullet from the unknown assailant's rifle struck him in the shoulder and flung him backwards. He hit the ground, breath expelled from his lungs with a loud blast and he lay there, moaning, the blood bubbling up from the wound.

He scanned the sky, looking for the face of God, for His mocking grin. This should not be happening. He had fought and killed and no one ever so much as winged him with a bullet. Now this. Out here, in the sweltering heat, with his best friend dead. How could it come to this? He rolled over onto his knees, clenched his teeth and stood up, a new resolve gripping every fiber of his body. He checked his gun again. Three shots. "Enough," he growled to himself.

Wild Eagle's wife cried out in fear as she craned her neck to see Mason, still alive, gun in hand. She sawed frantically at her man's bonds, then yelped her triumph as the ropes parted. Her husband stood up, rubbing his wrists, swept up the revolver and gripped her by the arm. "Go to the tepee, stay there, and keep the rifle pointed at the entrance. Do not move until I return."

"But I cannot leave you to this—"

"Go, Doe Eyes," he snapped, "before we both die."

She needed no further convincing and took off towards their worn, canvas and deerskin tent at a sprint, bent double, swerving from left to right. Wide Eagle watched her, half expecting another gunshot to come blasting out from nowhere, but nothing happened and he sighed loudly as she hurled herself full stretch and disappeared through the flap. He checked the pistol she'd given him, cocked the hammer and looked around for cover. Mason caught his eye and something passed between them. A coldness gripped Wild Eagle, causing him to stumble over to a scattering of rocks, needing to get away, get away from the horrors about to erupt. He half-expected the naked apparition some feet away to kill him. But nothing happened. Not yet.

A second man strode across the open ground, oblivious to danger, tall and straight, carbine gripped lazily in one hand. Wide Eagle could not make out the man's features, the large brimmed hat casting his face into deep shadow, but he could guess at the cruel eyes, the thin mouth, the look of a killer.

Wild Eagle crouched down behind the largest boulder, his body collapsing with relief. He still breathed, there remained a sliver of hope. He peered out from around the rock and held his breath, mouth clamped shut, eyes taking in every movement, every word.

* * *

Simms stopped and waited.

Mason turned, the revolver heavy in his hand, the sun like an anvil, beating down on his naked body. He stared, ran his tongue across dry lips.

"I know you," he said. "You were at Bovey."

"I've been everywhere you've been."

Mason frowned, cocked his head, tried to smile. But his lips were as cracked as sun-bleached bracken, all of the moisture sucked from them and they hurt. His attempt became nothing more than a slight upturning of his mouth's corners. "Is that right?" Simms nodded, just the once. "You been on my trail, ain't you, you stinking piece of shit."

Simms sighed. "You should never have taken the girl."

Mason frowned. "*The girl?*" He thought for a moment before his eyes slowly widened, understanding dawning. "Ah, I get it. The girl at the robbery, yeah? Elisabeth? She must be mighty important for you to keep on a-coming."

"She's safe now."

"Well, that's as maybe, but she won't always be that way. Maybe I have a mind to go back to the ranch, take up where I left off."

"Afraid not. Your time has just about run out."

Mason's mouth turned down at the corners, his body rigid, tense with indignation, anger. "Oh, you think so, eh? Think you can better me, is that it?" Mason shook his head. "Maybe you should think of things the other way, friend. I aim to kill you, for what you did to Newhart."

The tiniest look of surprise and Simms nodded. "He was a sorry son of a bitch anyway."

"Not as sorry as you are going to be, you bastard." Mason grinned. "Didn't anyone ever tell you – I'm blessed. No one can kill me."

"Why not find out if that's true?"

"You're mighty full of yourself. Who the fuck are you?"

"For Elisabeth, for her father, for all those you have killed, and…" he gestured with a finger towards the deerskin tepee, "for what you would have done to that girl."

They stared at each other, both men rigid, the slight breeze playing around with the dust, a buzzard arcing across the sky, unnoticed, its plaintive screech echoing across the plain.

The sun beat down, remorseless, hot enough to singe flesh, intense enough to cause sweat to evaporate, bright enough for the rays to bounce off the flat earth as if it were a mirror.

Mason peered deep into the other man's eyes. He knew about death, killing, suffering and pain. He'd lived a life in which he took what he wanted and if anyone crossed him, he would snuff them out as easily as a candle flame between thumb and forefinger. He shot his first man when he was just fourteen, a big man, loud-mouthed, working out of a railroad warehouse who slapped Mason across the face one morning for being lazy. Mason took the gun from the man's belt and shot him in the guts, point-blank range. He'd watched the man squirm and writhe on the ground and he liked what he saw.

But they ran him out of town. He never saw his family or friends again.

So he made his way and no one had bettered him. He grew arrogant and dismissive of others – their feelings, their opinions. He hardened his heart, never once allowing anyone in. Love and affection were alien concepts to him, his only friend the gun at his hip. And it was a friend that served him well. Hesitation was not a concept he recognized, he merely knocked down those who stood in his way.

This man, however, caused him to pause.

He'd faced many men, in fist fights, knife fights and gunfights. Big, small, strong and weak. He'd overcome them all, his single-minded desire to destroy lending him a kind of invulnerability. He dismissed pain and fear was unknown to him. This made him reckless, prone to acts of extreme violence the like of which his opponents had never experienced, and they wilted and died before him.

This man, however, brought something unknown to him.

Something he did not recognize, but guessed what it was.

Uncertainty.

He saw something, in the man's eyes. A latent fury, a simmering hatred to match his own. But controlled, where his was unfettered and wild.

He had never seen the like of it before in his life.

As he stood and stared at his opponent – rigid, motionless, eyes unblinking, the stance so relaxed – a tremor of something ran through Mason, across his back and down deep into his bowels.

Doubt.

He grunted, swatting the thoughts away like so many irritating flies and in a blur, Mason raised his gun. Unimpeded by a holster or waist-band, a flowing movement, almost graceful, with no warning, not even the merest flicker of changed expression in his eyes. As he brought up the gun, he dived to his right. Fast. Sudden.

And Simms. He saw it, knew, perhaps even before Mason, what was about to happen, and he swerved to his own right, and brought up the carbine, and shot Mason through the heart in mid-flight before any shots came in return.

Mason hit the dirt with a great thud, gun clattering from his fingers. He groaned and laid still, mouth working open and shut, but no sound escaped. His eyes rolled and an expression of abject horror and dis-belief crossed his face as the shadow moved across him, blanking out the sun. All of his senses focused in on the barrel of the big revolver, pointing directly at him. He didn't hear the boom from Simms's Colt Dragoon and he died, amongst the dust and the stones, naked and bloody, soon to be forgotten.

* * *

Wild Eagle spun out of sight, pressing his back against the rock. He'd watched, but continued to struggle over what he'd seen. The tall man with the carbine and the smoking revolver prevailed. A better option? He had no way of knowing. He gripped his gun. He doubted he could better such a man, but he would not roll over and die like a dog without a fight. Doe Eyes deserved every chance he could give her. So he raised himself up on one knee, aiming the revolver in both hands, eased back the hammer, and rested it across the top of the rock, to steady himself, give him an edge.

"Take it easy, chief," said the tall stranger, coming to a halt some ten paces away. He cradled the carbine across his chest, "if I wanted you dead, you'd be with these two shit-shovellers right now."

He waited. So did Wide Eagle. Nothing moved in that bleak, harsh landscape, the only sound the wind rattling across the dirt.

"I've been tracking them for longer than I care to remember. They're wanted in five counties and are the reason I'm here." He toed Mason in the ribs and glared into the dead man's eyes. "Excepting, this bastard has caused too much suffering, so in many ways I guess you could say, in the end, he has won." He put the carbine over his shoulder and looked across once more at Wild Eagle, who continued to train his revolver unerringly. "If you help me tie these two pieces of cow dung over my horse, I'll give you a share of the bounty. By the look of you, you're in sorry need of food… and clothes."

Wide Eagle recoiled a little, and looked down at himself, aware of his nakedness despite the large rock covering most of him from the man's gaze. He shot a glance to the tepee.

"She can come too," said the stranger, "but ask her to put the rifle away. It makes me kinda nervous."

Thirty-three

They tied the bodies to the sled instead of the horse and they rode together across the spreading ground, side by side, with the woman at her usual station, bringing up the rear.

When they made their first stop, Simms shared what food he had and he sat and watched them devouring the hard-tack and biscuits as if it was the most delicious meal on earth, which for them, it probably was.

They camped one more night under the stars and in the morning, when they stood and looked across the plain, a single trail of smoke told them Martinson's was close. As they set off on the last leg of their journey a distant rumble caused them to rein in their mounts and they listened, alert, watching broad belts of purple blue spreads across the sky. Colors mingled, undulated and changed as great forks of lightning lit them up. The temperature dropped, the horses whinnied.

"Dear God Almighty," said Simms, glancing across to Wide Eagle. "It's a storm!"

They gaped at one another and then, as Doe Eyes ran up to them to gaze towards the wonders developing overhead, they broke into laughter.

They saw Martinson in the doorway, beating an old carpet against the wall of his store, and Simms raised his hat and cried out. And Noreen appeared, looking fine in a white pinafore, blue blouse and dark grey skirt. Her face broke into a wide grin and as Simms steered his horse into the yard, she was there, running up to him, and the look in her eyes was the most beautiful thing he'd ever seen.

"Well, strike me down," said Martinson going over to the two bundled bodies. He shook his head. "Is this them?"

"It is."

Martinson shook his head and pushed his hat back onto his head. "I never thought I'd see the day. We've had such God-awful news." He watched Wild Eagle slide down from his pony and held the man's stare.

"This is Wild Eagle," said Simms, whose arm, as if by its own design, had slipped around Noreen's waist. She had her head on his chest. Martinson saw it, smiled, then nodded to the Native American.

Wild Eagle bowed slightly and Doe Eyes came up alongside and slipped her hand in his.

"Looks like you could all do with a good meal," said Martinson. "Noreen, could you perhaps prepare the table whilst I help get these bodies under cover?"

Noreen smiled up into Simms eyes and pressed him to her. "It'll be my pleasure."

Simms watched her go and, when she reached the door, she turned and gave him another smile and he felt that thrill run through his heart, the only pain he'd ever experienced which brought nothing but joy.

The men cut through the ropes holding the bodies and together they took them into the barn, laying them down, still covered in sack-cloth, amongst the straw.

"I would have liked to have seen his face," said Martinson.

"No you wouldn't," said Simms. "Best to think of him like this. A dead, faceless *thing*. Of no consequence."

"Yes," said Martinson, nodding his head briskly, "I can understand that."

They wandered back to the sled and Martinson took Simms by the elbow and led him away from the others.

"News came through along the wire, my friend. Your charge, Elisabeth Randall?" Simms held his breath. Martinson smiled. "She reunited with her father. It appears they will both be moving into their new home. The ranch where you first met her? Seems like the good general has got religion."

"Doesn't that beat all."

"But, I have to say, Detective, people won't take kindly to having Indians here. There's been some terrible incidents. Killings. Utes and Bannocks running amok, burning homesteads. Folks around these parts no longer differentiate, not that they ever did. But the deprivations suffered by so many, well…"

"I've witnessed them." A heavy rumble shook the very ground upon which they stood and both men looked skywards. "Once the rains come, we will all find some relief."

"I pray it is so."

"Don't fret none about Wild Eagle. He's suffered more than most and once his stomach is filled, he and his woman will go west."

"I'm glad to hear it. I would hate anything bad to befall them, not that much worse could happen after what Mason put them through. Or planned to do. Tavis has been visiting, bringing his usual merriment to the conversation. He brought news of the trail of killings, ending with the terrible gunfight over at Bovey. Garfield Smith has upped the reward, so I understand. It stands at a thousand dollars for Mason, half that for the other one."

"Dear God."

"I reckon you've earned yourself a small fortune here, detective."

Simms forced his tongue between his lips, deep in thought. Fifteen hundred dollars. More money than he had ever dreamed of. Enough to make a new life, to leave the past behind. Far behind.

Later they sat around the table and ate the meal Noreen prepared for them and the three of them stopped and gazed in amazement at Wide Eagle and Doe Eyes attacking the dumplings and gravy with a ferocity that belonged on the battlefield. Wild Eagle caught their stares and they all laughed.

It rained in the night, a tremendous thunderclap preceding a deluge so heavy it threatened to beat down the store roof. They stood under the veranda cover and watched the rain hitting the ground like bullets, ricocheting in every direction, the ground so hard, so dry, the water could not penetrate. Soon it seemed as if they were looking out over the surface of a lake.

Martinson had to shout to make himself heard, asking them if they wanted coffee. The natives declined, but Simms and Noreen both smiled and went back inside.

"I think the moment calls for one of these," said Martinson, after he'd poured the coffee. He passed across a thick, perfectly rolled cigar. Simms took it and breathed in the aroma, then bit off the end before accepting Martinson's match. He puffed on the smoke, leaned back in his chair, and allowed himself to breathe more easily than he had since alighting the train from Chicago all that time ago.

Later they sat and watched the rain again. It was less heavy now, easing into a steady, continuous downpour, the earth at last soaking up the surface water. Martinson talked about news from the west and east, how Mormons under Jacob Hamblin were building a defensive wall at Echo Canyon, that more troops were arriving daily at Fort Bridger, now almost rebuilt. Some were talking of an assault on Salt Lake City, others that peace would come well before such a thing occurred. Rumor and distortion. Hadn't it always been the way.

Martinson retired, the Native Americans bedding down in the barn beside the horses. And Simms sat out with Noreen close by and they talked with their eyes, and those words unspoken could fill volumes.

In the morning, they stood and waved as Wide Eagle and Doe Eyes set off once more across the prairie. Well supplied with food and grain, it was a joyous farewell.

"They seem such good people," said Noreen.

"I believe they are," said Simms. For the first time since he could remember, he did not wear his guns. "And so are we."

"Yes," she said.

Riders came, Garfield Smith at their lead, and he jumped down and embraced Simms as if he were a long, lost son. "The whole Territory owes you a great deal of gratitude, Mr. Simms." He pressed his lips together, the tears sprouting from his eyes. "Thank you."

Simms didn't know what to say and when he turned to Noreen she was crying too, but he recognized those tears for what they were – unbridled joy.

Gratitude.

A word he knew little of. Until now.

Garfield Smith led him into Martinson's store and there, at the counter, he counted out the money and Simms stared wide-eyed.

"You've done enough for us all so the least I can do is take the bodies across to Salt Lake," said Garfield Smith. "We'll bury them in the ground, unmarked, after we've filled in the papers with the U.S. Marshall. You stay here, where you're needed, my friend." He shook Simms's hand. "I've put in an extra two hundred, Mr. Simms. Seventeen hundred dollars."

Simms shook his head, numb with the shock of it all.

"I'll suspect you'll be heading off back east soon, to notify your agency."

"I…" Simms stumbled over his words. Thoughts of Chicago had never entered his mind these past few days. The idea that he may have to go back was not something to bring him much comfort.

Garfield Smith gave a small cough. "If you like, I can telegraph them the news. It's a godsend we can do such things now. If you decide to go back, please come and visit me at the ranch. You'll always be welcome." He repositioned his hat and was about to leave when something struck him, causing him to turn again, mouth twisted, deep in thought. "Detective… I may be crossing the line a little here, but… Well, damn it, if you *do* decide to stay, I have a plot of land. It's good grazing land, and what with the season changing and all, you could… well, what I'm trying to say is, why not consider staying in these parts? I think folk around here would be more than happy with such a decision and, hell's bells, you've deserved it. Think on it, my friend."

He thrust out his hand again and Simms took it, as if in a dream, and mumbled, "I shall."

When Greenfield Smith left, Simms noticed Noreen hovering in the corner. Her eyes were wide and full of expectation. Smiling, she drifted towards him. "Do you think you might decide to stay?"

He knew, as he looked at her face, so lovely and so expectant, that life had changed for the better and he made his decision, right there at that moment, with a heart swollen with joy.

Dear reader,

We hope you enjoyed reading *Unflinching*. Please take a moment to leave a review, even if it's a short one. Your opinion is important to us.

Discover more books by Stuart G. Yates at https://www.nextchapter.pub/authors/stuart-g-yates

Want to know when one of our books is free or discounted? Join the newsletter at http://eepurl.com/bqqB3H

Best regards,

Stuart G. Yates and the Next Chapter Team

The story continues in:
In The Blood by Stuart G. Yates

To read the first chapter for free, please head to:
https://www.nextchapter.pub/books/in-the-blood

About the Author

Stuart G Yates is the author of an eclectic mix of books, ranging from historical fiction through to contemporary thrillers. Hailing from Merseyside, he now lives in southern Spain, where he teaches history, but dreams of living on a narrowboat in Shropshire.

Unflinching
ISBN: 978-4-86747-312-2

Published by
Next Chapter
1-60-20 Minami-Otsuka
170-0005 Toshima-Ku, Tokyo
+818035793528
31th May 2021

Lightning Source UK Ltd.
Milton Keynes UK
UKHW012045090223
416722UK00004B/398

9 784867 473122